PARTL

In addition to being the director of such
classic films as *Whistle Down the Wind*, *The
Stepford Wives*, *King Rat* and *Seance on a Wet
Afternoon*, Bryan Forbes is the author of
several bestselling novels, notably *The
Endless Game*, together with works of
non-fiction. With his wife, Nanette
Newman, he divides his time between
England and Arizona.

BRYAN FORBES

Partly Cloudy

Mandarin

A Mandarin Paperback
PARTLY CLOUDY

First published in Great Britain 1995
by William Heinemann
This edition published 1995
by Mandarin Paperbacks
an imprint of Reed Books Ltd
Michelin House, 81 Fulham Road, London SW3 6RB
and Auckland, Melbourne, Singapore and Toronto

A CIP catalogue record for this title
is available from the British Library
ISBN 0 7493 1977 1

Printed and bound in Great Britain
by Cox & Wyman Ltd, Reading, Berkshire

For
India Rose, Archie and Tilly

'Partly cloudy, chance of blue skies later.'

Weather Report

One

During the run-up to that particular Christmas Eve Tony had convinced himself that the house was poised to go into a self-destruct mode rather like much of England. 1993 had been his own *annus horribilis* and he would not be sorry to see the back of it.

Opening the kitchen door to throw out a dead vole the cat had thoughtfully donated as its holiday offering, he heard an ominous thumping coming from the central heating boiler. The sounds seemed all the more menacing by virtue of the silence outside – the snow had arrived on seasonal cue for once, deadening the surrounding Buckinghamshire countryside. If the boiler gives out on us now, Tony thought, I may well emigrate. The previous Christmas a rogue dishwasher had inexplicably crunched all the wine glasses, and the year before that the oven had gone on the blink at a critical juncture, generating volcanic heat which had reduced the eighteen-pound goose to a charred corpse the size of a crow.

Having disposed of the vole he approached the

boiler cautiously, staring without comprehension at the quavering needle on the pressure gauge. What did it signify? It was a well-known fact that manufacturers deliberately programmed every machine to expire the second the guarantee ran out. So what action was demanded? He scrabbled about in the drawer meant to hold various instruction booklets but which contained nothing but a collection of old corks. After a further panic search he suddenly spotted the one for the boiler pinned to the message board above the telephone. The English section was torn and the only legible instructions were in Swedish. While he considered his options the boiler coughed twice then gave a long sigh somewhere in its innards. Tony backed away and in so doing slipped on a Brussels sprout carcass. Flinging out a hand to save himself he somehow managed to pull a very naked Christmas turkey off the counter. It hit the floor fractionally ahead of him, cushioning his fall, his cheek coming to rest against the clammy parson's nose. If this is the beginning, he thought, what is the end to be? At ground level he found himself staring at a motley collection of flaccid vitamin capsules; on average he dropped and lost one every day, his first waking hours being very hit or miss. When the children were little it had been an unwritten law that nobody talked to Daddy before ten o'clock. Daddy was scarcely human until then.

He lay there for a few moments, content to feel out of it all, but at length roused himself to the sense of time passing. Struggling upright, he hoisted the turkey up onto the counter. A feeling of infinite sadness swept over him as he forced himself to prod the headless bird back into shape, then limped into the living room intent on sharing his misfortunes.

'Sod it,' he said as he entered.

'Do what, darling?'

Kate, his wife of some twenty-five years, was perched on a step-ladder putting the finishing touches to the Christmas tree.

'I said, "sod it" because I just fell over. Probably done myself a permanent injury. The kitchen is like an assault course.'

If he was expecting sympathy he got none. 'The tree lights won't work,' Kate said, leaning at a perilous angle to drape a tinsel garland.

'Yes, well, the lights are going out all over Europe,' Tony growled.

'Try and jiggle them or something. Give the flex a shake, that sometimes works.'

'There was something I wanted to ask you. What was it? What have I been thinking about recently?'

'Haven't a clue, darling. There!' Kate paused to study her handiwork, then looked at him for the first time. 'Are you going to change before everybody gets here?'

'Why, what's wrong with what I've got on?'

'Nothing, dear.'

Familiar with the tone of voice Kate used when

things were not to her liking – honeyed but with a hard centre – Tony examined his appearance in the mirror over the fireplace. True he looked his forty-eight years, but he saw nothing else that deserved criticism. His hair, which he had forgotten to have trimmed in the pre-Christmas mêlée, was flecked with grey, but at least it was still there. 'I thought this plaid shirt was suitably festive.'

'Yes, it's nice, darling, but it's got a tear in it and a stain down the front.'

'How can you see from there?'

'It came back from the laundry with a tag saying they couldn't get it out.'

'Oh. I thought that was part of the pattern. Would you rather I changed into black tie?'

'Don't be silly. I just want you to look your best, that's all. What time are you fetching your father?'

'Shortly. Don't keep getting off the subject. I came in to ask you something, now it's gone again. What was it?'

'Watch,' Kate said, still intent on decorating the tree, 'if I wobble on the ladder the lights flicker on and off. It's the same with my radio in the bedroom. When I walk away from that the station changes. Was it to do with the food?'

'Was what to do with the food?'

'Whatever you're trying to remember. I just hope I've ordered enough of everything. Last year your father complained he was hungry all the time.'

4

'No, not food. Not the boiler, although that's sounding bilious. Not the cat . . . it was . . . ' He stared around the room, his eyes coming to rest on the bookcase where the Christmas cards were displayed. 'I've got it! Did we send a card to those people?'

'I didn't send any cards. You did the cards, I did the presents.'

'All right. Well, did I?'

'Did you what?'

'Send them one?'

'Who?'

'You know, that couple we met in France last summer?'

Kate stretched to place an angel on the top of the tree. 'France,' she repeated, vagueing off again. 'France?'

'You remember. They sat next to us on the beach, smothered in oil.'

'Polluted, you mean?'

'No, listen! Stop that for a moment and listen. You must remember them. She was so burnt she looked like the last alligator bag in Asprey's, and he wore very dodgy bikini briefs. They took us out to dinner and we exchanged addresses, remember?'

Kate shook her head. 'Vaguely.'

'She was Guccied-up, looked like a walking tackroom when she was dressed, and he was a virtual midget, we said he reminded us of Toulouse Lautrec.'

'French were they?'

'No, Golders Green. In the rag trade.'

'Sorry, darling, can't help you. Be a dear and fiddle with the lights, will you? The man in the shop said to twist their little necks.'

'He probably meant children.' Tony eyed the flex warily. 'Are they safe?'

'You wired the plug.'

'You realise, don't you, that the entire wiring in this house is thirty years old and liable to go at any moment? You don't seem to appreciate we're living on the edge.' Tony traced the flex to the wall socket, made sure it was switched on, then gave a tentative jerk. Nothing happened.

'Gently! Otherwise the decorations will fall off.'

He shook the flex again. This time the lights fluttered into life for a few seconds.

'Brilliant, darling. That worked, whatever you did.'

Tony gave another shake. The lights came on and stayed on.

'Cross your fingers and walk away slowly.'

'The point I was trying to make,' Tony said with that maddening persistence that had often tried their marriage, 'they sent us one.'

'You're not still on that, are you?'

'Yes. This could be the beginning of Alzheimer's. I just have to solve it, otherwise I won't be able to write.'

'Well, you couldn't write tonight anyway. I'm sure even Proust took Christmas Eve off.'

'Here, I'll find it.' He went to the bookcase and

6

selected one of the cards. 'It says "Masses of holiday love from Ticky and Tiny". Does that ring a bell?'

'No.'

'You don't care, do you, if my mind's going?'

Kate came down from the step-ladder and surveyed her handiwork. 'That's finally it. What d'you think?'

'Why have you stuck that up again?'

'What?'

'That ju-ju thing on the top.'

'My angel, you mean?'

'Yes. It looks diseased.'

'Well, it's old,' Kate said. 'And I'm very attached to it. Don't be horrid about it, I've put it on the tree ever since the children were born.'

The lights flickered and went out again. 'You were ripped off with those things,' Tony said. 'Everybody gets ripped off at Christmas. Christmas is one long scam. Well, I'm not going to risk it. I shall leave them for Roger to sort out. He's the mechanical genius in the family and if he electrocutes himself, tough titty, it'll be the best start to Christmas we've ever had.'

'Oh, darling, don't go off Roger before he even gets here. Try and enjoy it for my sake. It's only for a couple of days.'

'I've always been off Roger. I've never had the faintest glimmer of sibling love. Last year the couple of days stretched to four because he was legless most of the time and Virginia can't drive.'

'Vanessa. You always get her name wrong.'

7

'Well, it's the Bloomsbury connection that confuses me.'

'Roger's not that bad. You have to admit he's very generous with his presents.'

'If you like ostentation,' Tony said. He helped himself to a whisky.

'You'll be legless if you start drinking now. What've we got Roger this year?'

'I haven't got him anything. The arrangement, as you reminded me, was I did the cards, you took care of the presents.'

'No. I said I'd get all the others, and you said you'd do Roger because he's so difficult to buy for and you didn't trust my taste. That's what you said.'

'I don't remember saying that.'

'Well, you did. So, now what? We can't leave him out, we'll just have to rewrap one of ours. Open the one from the Leeches.' She pointed to one of the parcels piled around the base of the tree.

'You serious?'

'Yes. We can't leave him out.'

'I don't believe any of this.' Tony ripped off the festive wrapping, then stared in shock at what was revealed – a framed photograph of Mr and Mrs Leech holding their Pekinese. The dog was noticeably suffering from catarrh and wearing a miniature T-shirt with the words 'Happy Christmas Jesus' embroidered on it.

'How gross can you get?' he exclaimed. 'People like

8

the Leeches should be put down together with their hideous dog. Look at it!'

'Yes. But then taste was never their middle name. Try another one.'

'We can't open every bloody parcel.'

'All right, well what's your solution? Have you got something tucked away we could give him? Something you don't want. I know! What about that pullover?'

'Which pullover?'

'The one . . . the green one with yellow bands on the sleeves.'

'You gave me that.'

'I know.'

'For my last birthday.'

'Yes, but you hate it.'

'No, I don't.'

'Well, you've never worn it.'

'I've been saving it. God, you're like a collector from Oxfam. I don't want to give that away.'

'This is crisis time,' Kate said firmly. 'And don't get upset. I've bought you another one for Christmas.'

'Oh, great! Now you've told me. I shan't have any surprises.'

'Yes, you will. It's just one of my presents.'

'How many have you bought me then?'

'Three . . . well, two now.'

'But I've only got you one.'

9

'Doesn't matter. I'm sure yours is much nicer than any of mine.'

'Makes me look mean. The family are bound to remark on it, you know how they love to score Brownie points. First thing Vanessa does is count all the cards.' He parodied a county accent: ' "Fancy, you've only had forty-two cards this year. We had over eighty, including one from the Chancellor of the Exchequer." '

'Darling, just go along with it, for my sake. She means well. Look at the time. Is that clock right? Can't be five already, can it? I must go and do my face, they'll all start arriving soon. I'll wrap your sweater and do a tag. You could help by clearing up all this rubbish and making sure the fires are okay. Don't want your father saying he's got hypothermia like last year.' She took one last, backward look at the tree. 'D'you think it looks good?'

'Yes, looks great.' Left to himself, a sense of *déjà vu* swept over him: despite his outward cynicism, he found something infinitely touching about the way in which Kate exhausted herself every year preparing for the family rituals which seldom lived up to her expectations. She cared so much about tradition, giving the entire house a Dickensian look; each succeeding year she brought out the hoarded mementoes of other Christmases so that in the end corners of every room were decorated with the serendipity of childhoods past. Why am I so uncharitable, he thought,

10

when it all means so much to her? As he bent to gather up the spare tinsel and torn wrapping paper, the tree lights came on. He experimented, reversing his actions several times, like a film being run backwards and forwards, alternately bending and straightening. The lights reacted in concert – first on, then off again. 'Stupid bloody things,' he said aloud.

At that moment the phone rang. When he picked up an operator asked, 'Are you Chalfont 74220?'

'Yes.'

'I have a Martin Chivers phoning from an Oxford call box who wishes you to pay for the call. Will you accept the charges?'

'Yes, I guess so.'

'Thank you. Go ahead caller.'

Their son came on the line. 'Dad, I heard that. Why did you hesitate?'

'It's the Christmas mood I'm in. We thought you'd be here by now.'

'I've broken down.'

'Haven't had an accident, have you?'

'No, Dad, just the fan belt conked out, but the AA's on the way to fix it. I just wanted to let you and Mummy know we'll be late.'

'Right. Well, that was thoughtful of you. Is Patricia with you?'

There was a pause before Martin answered. 'Evelyn, Dad.'

'And who is Evelyn, might I ask?'

There was another pause and Tony was conscious of a whispered exchange at the other end of the line. When Martin spoke again his voice was buttered. 'I would have mentioned it before, Dad, but everything happened in a bit of a rush.'

'Be more specific.'

'Between Pat and me. Difficult to explain right now, but the fact is we couldn't make a go of it, so we decided to . . . well, you know . . . '

'You ditched her in other words.'

'Not exactly. We just called it a day.'

'I see, and now you're bringing Evelyn instead, is that what you're trying to tell me?' Pack-ice had crept into Tony's voice. He and Kate had suffered, entertained, given bed and board to half a dozen Patricias and Evelyns during the time Martin had been up at Oxford ostensibly studying for a degree.

'If that's okay?'

'Well Mummy would certainly be very disappointed not to see you, so I imagine it will have to be. Look, since I'm paying for this call let's not stretch it out. Get the car fixed and for God's sake drive carefully and arrive in one piece.'

He hung up abruptly, annoyed that he had allowed his anger to show. Whenever Martin turned up with a new girlfriend he found he was unable to suppress basic fears. Jenny, their daughter, he was not so worried about; she was married to a serving soldier and so far the marriage seemed to be working. Despite Martin's denials that he wasn't casually promiscuous and didn't do drugs – 'well a little grass, perhaps, but doesn't everybody? Never the hard stuff, I promise' – Tony remained unsure. The young lied so easily and the warnings about Aids that he tried to drive home inevitably sounded like the usual parental dirge – platitudes from a middle-aged reactionary which were automatically discounted.

Disgruntled at the prospect of having to welcome a total stranger into their midst, he went to the foot of the stairs and shouted up to Kate. 'That was Martin on the phone. He's not bringing Patricia, he's bringing somebody called Evelyn.'

'Can't hear you. Say again.'

'Doesn't matter. It's bad news, it'll keep.'

Collecting up the tree debris he went into the kitchen to dispose of it and found the cat licking the turkey. He bundled the baleful animal outside and locked the cat flap, then thought, does it really matter? We're going to roast the bloody thing. At least the cat kills by instinct, we just gorge ourselves celebrating a pagan ritual.

The front doorbell rang and he stood stock still, listening, hoping it wasn't yet another band of carol singers; once in David's fair city they had presumably raised dulcet voices in tune, but that gift seemed to have died out in Buckinghamshire. Deciding he was safe from a further rendering of 'The Holly and the

Ivy', he went to the door and was confronted by his only brother, Roger.

A year older and a good three inches taller than himself, Roger was wearing what was, for him, casual clothes; that is to say he looked like somebody assembled from a 1960 mail-order catalogue. In addition he had grown his hair in the interval between their last reunion and now sported a ponytail which gave him the appearance of a faded pop musician rather than the chartered accountant he really was. The overall effect unnerved Tony.

'Ah! you made it!' he blurted after a momentary falter. 'How were the roads? Seems to have stopped snowing at last.'

'Yes, in places,' Roger said. 'Traffic was appalling, of course. Contra-flows everywhere and forests of those bloody cones. They must be the only growth industry in this country.'

Tony looked past him. 'No Vanessa and the kids?'

'No.'

'Ah! . . . Coming later under their own steam, are they?'

Roger pursed his lips and blinked several times. 'No.'

'No, don't know why I said that really, because Vanessa doesn't drive, does she?'

'You may as well know straight away, they're not coming at all.'

'Ah! . . . Not ill, are they?'

14

'Van and I have split up. I'm allowing her to divorce me.'

'Ah!' Tony said for the fourth time.

'Are you going to let me stand here in the freezing cold while you endlessly say "Ah"?'

'No, of course not. Sorry. Come in.'

'Thank you.' Roger deposited his small overnight case in the hallway and removed his topcoat, folding it neatly. 'Have any of the others arrived?'

'Er, not yet, no, you're the first.'

'Good. That's a relief. Wanted to break the news to you without the others.'

'I can imagine. Come into the warm. Expect you need a drink.' Tony led the way into the living room. 'What'll it be, the usual?'

'I won't, thank you,' Roger said stiffly.

'Nothing? You serious?'

'I've sworn off it.'

'Ah! Have you? . . . Sorry, didn't mean it to come out like that. Well, if you don't object, I haven't and in view of your news, I feel in need of one. Curiously enough, somehow I hadn't allowed for sharing Christmas with a sober divorcee.' His attempt to thaw the atmosphere had no noticeable effect.

'Trust you to make light of it. You don't approve obviously?'

'Of abstinence or divorce? Can I think about it?'

'I shouldn't have come,' Roger said, warming his ass in front of the fire. He took out a silk handkerchief and wiped a drip from the end of his nose. 'I might have guessed what your reaction would be.'

'Don't be silly, what are brothers for if not to shock each other? . . . Rog, put yourself in my place, you can't blame me for being surprised by what you've just told me. I know I write fiction for a living, but this isn't a plot that would have come easily to mind. Why? How? What the hell brought all this on suddenly?'

'Not suddenly. There's been a worm in the bud for some time. I'm surprised you and Kate didn't notice.'

'Why would we? We only see you both at Christmas. And anyway, being country mice, far from the city lights, we're pretty dense about such things.'

'What have city lights got to do with it? You think marriages never fail in these rural parts?'

'No, I don't think that.'

'So why say it?'

'Rog, don't get huffy with me. All I meant was, as far as we knew, you both seemed well suited and reasonably happy.'

'It was an act we kept up for the sake of appearances. In my line of business clients like to feel they are handled by somebody who is family-orientated.'

'Really? You used to tell me your main concern was to keep your clients out of jail . . . So do I take it you've found somebody else?'

'No. Typical of you to think sex would be the reason. There are other things in life.'

'My apologies. Was it Van then? Has she gone off?'

'Good God no!'

'Well, don't say it so emphatically. She's still a very attractive woman. So what then?'

'I needed to find myself.'

'Don't we all? Roger, let's not play pass the parcel. Just as long as you're not going to confess you've come out of the closet, because that I couldn't take.'

'Thank you. I expected a cheap jibe like that. It wouldn't occur to you, would it, that some of us are capable of having a spiritual experience that changes our entire lives?'

'Since we're talking about you, frankly no.'

'Just proves how little you know me.'

'Well, that's true. I've never known you. I'm closer to my publisher than I am to you, something which, believe it or not, I regret.'

'I happen to have been born again.'

Tony struggled to keep his face under control.

'That obviously strikes you as amusing,' Roger said. 'Well, it isn't remotely amusing to me. Finding God is a serious matter.'

'You've found God?'

'Yes.'

'Well, congratulations. I can't even find myself a literary agent.'

'There you go again. You can't resist being cynical, can you?'

'No, I can't in the circumstances. It's obviously

17

incredibly dense of me, but I fail to see why finding God has to be incompatible with a happy marriage. I thought that was the Christian ethic.'

'Did I say I had become a born-again Christian?'

'Haven't you?'

'No. I intend to follow Islam.'

Tony choked on his drink. 'Does that mean you'll be burning copies of *The Satanic Verses* in Hampstead Garden Suburb?'

'I'm going,' Roger said. 'It cost me an effort to come here on my own. I did it for Kate's sake more than yours, since I know how much store she sets by a family Christmas, but I might have guessed you'd take this attitude.'

'Sorry, sorry, I won't say another word. But just promise me one thing ... when the old man gets here, please, whatever else, keep off religion, especially your new-found faith. Ever since the Gulf War anything East of Suez rattles his dentures.'

'Well, he'll have to know sooner or later,' Roger replied. 'Father must learn to live in the real world.'

'Why? He never has so far.'

Further discussion was interrupted as Kate returned carrying the newly-wrapped pullover intended for Roger. She tucked this behind a cushion on the sofa before greeting him.

'Merry Christmas, Roger dear. How lovely to see you, it's been far too long. You haven't got a drink. Tony, your brother hasn't got a drink.'

'He doesn't want one,' Tony said quickly.

'Course he wants one after a long drive. What would you like, Roger, dear?' She went to the drinks table, then suddenly paused. 'Where're Vanessa and the girls?'

Tony jumped in again. 'They couldn't come.' He contorted his face behind Roger's back, but Kate did not latch on.

'Oh, no! Why not? They haven't caught this Chinese flu, have they? So many people we know have come down with it, and apparently it's very nasty this year. We've missed it so far, touch wood.'

This time Roger got in ahead of Tony. 'No, they're fine, but they're spending Christmas with Van's parents this year.'

This time Kate noticed Tony's face language and returned it with her own grimace before responding. 'Oh, I see. Unlike her not to have told me.'

'That was my fault. I should have rung. It all happened in a bit of a rush, I'm afraid.'

'We'll miss the children. I was so looking forward to seeing them, but nice for Vanessa's parents.' Her disappointment was obvious. She looked from Tony to Roger, sensing the strained atmosphere and hoping one of them would explain the tension, but all Roger said was: 'Look, I'll go and freshen up if you don't mind. Had a long journey and I came straight from the office.'

'Yes, of course, I'm sure you need to unpack,' Kate

answered, still baffled by what was going on. 'I've put you in your usual room, and you can use the second bathroom. You know your way around.'

'Yes. Good. I'll spruce myself up then, see you in a while.'

Kate waited until he was safely out of earshot before rounding on Tony. 'What on earth's going on, giving me all those looks?'

'Sit down. Have a drink.'

'I can't sit down, I've got to stuff the turkey. And you haven't changed.'

'Forget that. *Sit down.*' He poured her a drink.

'I don't want a drink.'

'You *do* want a drink, believe me. Even as we speak our turkey is already, metaphorically, stuffed.' He thrust the glass into her hand. 'Have a good swig.'

Speaking quietly and deliberately, as to a small child, he enumerated the state of play. 'One, Vanessa and the girls are not coming because; two, she and Roger are getting divorced; three, Roger is off the juice and; four, he has heard the call of the Ayatollahs and intends to follow the dictates of Islam. Did you get all that or would you like me to repeat it?'

Kate slumped down on the arm of the sofa. 'Don't, I can't bear it! . . . Are you making it up?'

'Cross my heart. And keep your voice down. What we have to do is figure out a way to keep most of it from Pop. He'll have to know about Vanessa, because her not being here is going to be obvious.'

'Oh, God, and after all the trouble I've gone to.'

'Well, listen, it's only for a short time, mercifully ... Oh, and stay sitting, because there is one last gem. Our son telephoned to say he's broken down on the motorway ... don't panic, he hasn't had an accident, he's quite all right ... but instead of bringing Patricia as we expected, he is now bringing somebody called Evelyn.'

'Evelyn?'

'That's what I said.'

'Who the hell's Evelyn?'

'No idea.'

'How could he? He drives me mad sometimes, treats this place like a hotel, and at Christmas of all times.'

'It's the season of rejection. The suicide rate doubles in Finland.' His attempt to make light of it failed.

'Well, we're not in Finland,' Kate sniffed. 'And why has Roger done his hair like that? Looks ridiculous on somebody his age. I don't know why he bothered to come, he's going to put a damper on everything, what with his situation, and stupid Martin bringing somebody we've never met. I don't know, I give up.'

'Don't give up. We'll just have to make the best of it.'

'Will we ever split up?'

'Never at Christmas, I'd always wait until it was

warmer.' Tony kissed her. 'Don't be an idiot, of course not. You're much too sexy.'

'I won't be sexy for ever, then you'll go off me. It doesn't matter so much for men.'

'What doesn't?'

'Looks. Men get more attractive as they get older. I remember something Vanessa said to me last year. We were up in the bedroom and she said, "I can't be bothered any more". I thought then, "Big Mistake". That's why I do my exercises. I don't want to end up with a hump on my back looking like all those old women in shopping malls pushing walkers.'

'That's never going to happen. Now stop upsetting yourself.' He kissed her again and kept his hand on her breast, thinking how lucky he was compared to Roger, or even Martin, especially Martin who was still looking for the bluebird of happiness. 'We'll get through this, we just have to hang in there for two days, and afterwards I'll take you away somewhere – Paris, or Skegness if you prefer. I'm told Skegness is jumping in the winter and I can get a special rate.'

There was another ring at the doorbell. This time it was Jenny, their daughter, cheeks flushed from the cold, dressed in a scarlet coat cut military style with bright brass buttons.

'Am I late? Everybody else here?' she asked, kissing her father.

Embracing her Tony tasted the perfume on her skin

– a trace of lily of the valley like the memory of summers past. He was always unprepared for her beauty and now as she moved past him to greet her mother he saw them both as two indivisible parts of his life, so different and yet so alike in many ways.

'No, you're almost the first.'

'What a sensational coat, darling,' Kate exclaimed. 'Where did you find it?'

'Andy sent me the money and I splurged, gave Ralph Lauren a thrashing.'

'If you hadn't told me,' Tony said, 'I'd have thought it was Army surplus.'

'Oh, ha ha. You all right, Mummy?'

'Yes, darling, why?'

'You look as though you've been crying.'

'I've been peeling onions. That coat looks great on you, can I try it on?' The coat changed hands.

'Any chance Andy will make it home for Christmas?' Tony asked.

'No, worse luck. They cancelled all leave and put them on full alert.'

Kate stopped admiring the coat in the hall mirror. 'But I thought the IRA had promised a ceasefire over the holidays? That's what they said on the news.'

'Well, I don't know Mummy. He has to do what he's told.'

'Oh, dear. What with Roger's situation . . . '

'What? What situation?'

'Shh!' Tony said. 'Let her get into the warm first.'

'No, tell me,' Jenny said. 'What's happened with Roger?'

'A domestic *crise*.'

'Why're you whispering?'

Tony pointed a finger upstairs and walked her into the living room. 'He and Van are getting divorced.'

Jenny shrugged. 'That doesn't surprise me. I saw that coming. I know he's your brother, Daddy, but let's face it, he's always been a mega arsehole.'

'Jenny!' her mother admonished.

'Well, he is. If you ask me, Van should have left him ages ago. I know I would have.' The subject bored her, she dismissed it. 'Doesn't the tree look great as usual! And you've put the angel up.'

'Are the rest of your things in the car?' Tony said. 'I'll get them.'

'Well, don't peek inside any of the plastic bags, Daddy.'

'As if I would.'

'You always cheat and then you don't have any surprises Christmas morning.'

'Then go and get your father,' Kate said, 'otherwise he'll be in a state.'

The moment they were alone Kate returned to the topic that most concerned her. 'Don't worry, darling. I'm sure he'll be all right.'

'I don't care if he is or isn't. I'm just sorry for Van.'

'I meant Andy.'

'Mummy,' Jenny said firmly. 'I've lived with it on

and off for years now. It's Andy's third tour and he says apart from the boredom it's safer than travelling on the M25. Of course I'd rather he was back in England and we were spending Christmas together, but it's his life, the one he wanted and I settled for.'

'Oh, I know, dear, I know. Just that . . . well . . . '

There was a moment's silence between them, a helpless sort of silence, and it seemed to Kate that everything had stopped, as though time had been suspended. She remembered when Jenny was a small child she had always known, no matter what distance separated them, when something bad was about to happen.

Two

When Tony arrived at his father's small flat in Iver Heath he was touched to find the old man already wearing his overcoat and trilby hat.

'Everything okay, Pop?'

'Yes. Are we off then?'

His dentures were not a perfect fit which sometimes made the odd word come out with a hiss.

'I'll leave one light on, just in case. You never know.'

Looking around the small living room, Tony thought how little there was worth stealing: the odd piece of war-time utility furniture his father still clung to, a few ornaments and framed pictures of the grandchildren together with the retirement clock that seldom told the correct time. It was a life encapsulated in a time warp, as rigid as the patterned wallpaper and carpet. Many times Tony and Kate had gently suggested changes, offering to get the old man a more comfortable armchair, some brighter curtains, but without success: he liked it the way it was, a last link with the past, and they had finally given up.

On the outward journey Tony had tried to decide the best way of handling Roger's bombshell. The pending divorce was tricky enough, bound to concern the old man who held very conservative views about marriage, but explaining the yellow brick road to Mecca was something else.

The problem was that his father's life was built around half-comprehended bits of information gleaned from snippets of news that seldom, if ever, interlocked. This had the effect of making strangers bewildered; they could never be quite sure when he was being deliberately humorous or merely testing their reactions. Tony had often seen the reflection of the firing squad come into strangers' eyes when they were exposed to one of his father's malapropisms for the first time.

A widower for the past seven years, Chivers Sr, always known as 'Pop' within the family, was still a handsome man although, no longer restricted since his wife's death, he had changed his eating habits, proud of his independence now that he had mastered the art of heating TV dinners, and had put on too much weight for his age. He had never been close to Tony as a child, being more drawn to Roger's staid personality, and later the fact that

Roger had chosen to follow a profession he approved of and could understand. He had never been able to fathom what Tony did: writing, as a means of making a living, was a foreign country to him. Whenever Tony produced a new novel his father made an effort to show interest, probing for clues, like a dentist looking for decay, in an effort to understand what Tony's life consisted of, but the final answer escaped him. Tony knew that some of the subjects he wrote about shocked his father, though the old man never made direct references to anything, confining himself to generalities such as 'Did well, did it, people like to read that sort of thing?' The only printed matter he studied with any intensity was his daily tabloid, garnering from it a collection of prejudices that he hoarded until he had a captive audience. During his own working life his father had always had a regular salary, so the idea of somebody self-employed, working at home, with no guarantee of where the next cheque was coming from, defeated him. Tony remembered how, when a child, he had observed the weekly accounting: the portioning of the money – so much for housekeeping, so much for insurance and the utilities, all put into separate compartments of the black cash box he kept, incongruously it now seemed, in the kitchen.

Once seat-belted into the Volvo – the belt only just encompassing his girth – he immediately asked the question that Tony was hoping to avoid.

'How are the children?'

'I think they're fine, Pop.' He plunged, choosing the easiest revelation to begin with. 'You won't be seeing the other grandchildren this year. Vanessa's taking them to her parents. I expect they wanted their turn. You'll see Roger, though. He's here.'

'Come without them, has he? Oh, dear. That is a blow. I've brought all the kids presents.'

'Well, they'll have something to look forward to after Christmas.'

'Won't be the same without everybody there. Your mother and I always had a full house. Oh, dear, wasn't expecting that.' His father was silent for a while then, unexpectedly, said: 'Trouble there, is there?'

No flies on Pop, Tony thought. 'How d'you mean, trouble?'

'Between Roger and her?'

'Roger did mention they weren't getting on too well. Still, all marriages go through bad patches, don't they?'

Another silence, longer this time, and Tony attempted to change the subject. He pointed to a shopping precinct which was still crowded. 'Some people are leaving it late to do last-minute shopping,' but this did not have the desired effect.

'Damn ridiculous. People have to make a go of it,' his father said, sucking in his breath. 'Stick it out. Make the best of it. Your mother could be a difficult woman at times, but we stuck it out, love.' He had always used the word 'love' as a term of endearment, regardless of age or sex. 'Has he got some fancy woman tucked away?'

'I don't think it's that, Pop. He's probably going through a mid-life crisis, takes some men that way.'

'Never took me that way, though I wasn't without my chances.' The word 'chances' struck Tony as having a mysterious ring and it occurred to him that he had never before thought of his father as a philanderer.

Trying to steer the conversation into less emotional waters, Tony switched to a topic that usually engaged his father's interest. 'Any luck with the football pools this season?'

'No. My teams have let me down every week. Can't understand it.'

For as long as Tony could remember his father had followed a system of his own that he insisted would one day produce a jackpot. It never had, but his faith in it never faltered.

'I tell you who is coming. Jenny's invited a couple of her friends for tomorrow – two American boys she works with. I guess she felt in need of some company her own age when Andy's leave was cancelled.'

'Cancelled, eh? Pity, pity. What about Martin?'

'Oh, yes. With a new girlfriend.'

'Got a new one, has he? He's a lad, our Martin. What's this one called?'

'Evelyn.'

'Evelyn, eh?' his father echoed, giving her name a curious intonation. 'I shall have to look her over then.'

'Well,' Tony said as he turned into the driveway, 'despite missing Andy and Vanessa, I'm sure we'll still have a good time.' When he had taken his father's things up to the bedroom, he rejoined him in the study to find the old man transfixed in front of his computer.

'Still writing are you?'

'Have to pay the gas bills, Pop.'

'These things write the words, do they?'

'Sort of. I have to think of them first.'

'By the way,' his father said, shifting abruptly into another gear, 'where's the dog? Haven't seen the dog.' His abrupt changes of subject had always been legend within the family.

'Fred died, Pop, remember?'

'Died, did he? Yes, they have a habit of that when they get older.'

Work that one out, Tony thought. 'Cat,' he said. 'We've got a cat called Emily.' But his father had moved on.

'You know what's going to happen, don't you, when they finally open that Channel Tunnel? We're going to be swamped with rabies, you mark my words. It should never have been allowed.' Then, as Tony poured him a large sweet sherry, he moved on yet again. 'I read now they're not going to let us buy cucumbers unless they're straight.'

'Really? Who said that, Pop? Cheers. Happy Christmas.'

'Why, those Euro people in Brussels. Damn Tommy-rot, I don't hold with it. Where're the others?'

'I expect Roger'll be down in a minute and Jenny's helping her mother in the kitchen.'

'And of course he's still there.' Tony waited for the interpretation. 'That Soddam man. Should have finished him when they had a chance.' The combination of the sherry which he had downed like water and his low level of tolerance towards anything foreign produced a creeping redness on his neck. 'What d'you make of it all?'

'I've given up, Pop. Don't even watch the news any more. Too depressing.'

'I wish I was in charge, I know what I'd do. Half the politicians should be in jail. And I'd do away with the Archbishop of Canterbury.'

Tony turned away to put another log on the fire, unable to trust his face. Where did all the pent-up rage come from? The enigma of his father, who had not been a bad parent, merely distant, a figure in a childhood landscape seen from afar, was something he had never been able to solve. On several occasions he had tried to put aspects of his father's personality into his novels, but without success. He seemed too large for the page or perhaps the same things that joined them set them apart. That awful expression 'bonding' which the Americans used conjured up a sickly mixture of James Barrie and A. A. Milne from which he had always shied. He did not want to bond with his father, he wanted to understand him.

At that moment they were joined by Roger and, rather than get involved, Tony took the opportunity to escape. 'You two have a chat, I'll just check whether Kate wants any help.'

'I was looking forward to seeing the girls,' he heard his father say as he left. Before he could reach the kitchen he heard a car draw up outside and went to investigate. As the headlights were extinguished he made out his son's battered TR7 which had slid the last few yards and come to a stop with its front wheels resting in a bed of dank hydrangeas, the remaining spent blooms balled with snow.

'Sorry about that, Dad,' Martin said as he emerged. 'But at least we made it.'

'It's time you put that old bus on the scrap heap,' Tony said. 'Has it got any tread left on the tyres?'

'Goes like a bomb usually. Just doesn't like this cold weather. Can't part with her, she's a collector's item.'

Another figure struggled out of the passenger seat and took a few timid steps on the icy path.

'Oh, Dad, this is Evelyn.' Martin grabbed at her as

Evelyn nearly slipped on the ice. Her face was partially obscured by a sweater wrapped around her head and it wasn't until she came under the driveway lights that Tony got a proper look at her. She wasn't anything like he had expected, bearing in mind his son's usual selection. 'Neat' was the first word he would have put to her. Little make-up, a pleasantly attractive rather than beautiful face, with high cheekbones and lovely eyes. What surprised him most was the fact that, unlike those that had gone before her, she wasn't anywhere near Martin's own age. He guessed her to be in her early thirties. He put out a helping hand until she reached the safety of the porch, then hesitated a fraction too long before bending to kiss her cold cheek.

'Hello, Evelyn. Glad you're joining us. Let's get you inside and thaw you out. I don't suppose Martin's pride and joy has a heater.'

'No, it doesn't,' she said. 'It's so nice of you and Mrs Chivers to let me spend Christmas with you.' She spoke in a quiet, cultivated voice.

'You're very welcome.' Now as she removed the sweater around her head, she revealed stylishly short-cropped hair. It was impossible for him to guess at her shape for she was swathed in a variety of sweaters under her coat. 'Come on in quickly and get warm,' he said. Martin struggled past him with two suitcases and whispered, 'Thanks, Dad. Sorry if I took you and Mummy unawares.'

34

'Well, you show Evelyn her room and I'll go and tell Mummy you've arrived safely. She's been worried about you. Make sure Evelyn's got everything she wants and show her where the bathroom is.'

He watched them start upstairs, then hurried into the kitchen.

'He's here,' he announced. 'All in one piece.'

'Oh, that's a relief. And is . . . with him?'

'Yes.'

'And?'

Tony lowered his voice, although there was little need since the extractor fan was going at full blast. 'Seems very nice. Older than the others.'

Kate stopped what she was doing, her hands smeared with stuffing. 'How much older?'

'Well, I didn't immediately ask her for her birth certificate . . . thirty or thereabouts.'

'Oh, one foot in the grave, Daddy,' Jenny said. 'My brother the toy boy.'

'But, I mean is she tarty?'

'The current buzz word is "slapper", Mummy,' Jenny said.

'I don't know what that means.'

'Neither do I,' Tony said. 'No, she's not a bit tarty, quite the reverse. You'll see for yourself in a minute.'

'Where did he find her? Did he say on the phone?'

'No.'

'Jenny, you go up and say hello, then come back

and tell me what you think. I want to tidy myself before I meet her. And just look at Roger's room while you're up there. Make sure it's okay.'

'Well, it won't be, will it?'

'What d'you mean?'

'I don't suppose it's facing Mecca.'

'Jenny! Those jokes are out,' Tony said.

'Pity Andy's going to miss all this. He's going to call around now, so let me answer the phone if it rings. And by the way, Daddy, I haven't gone teetotal, so how about a drink for the kitchen help when I come down?'

'Did I hear somebody mention a drink?' Martin said from the doorway. He stood aside to reveal Evelyn.

'Mummy, this is Evelyn. My mother and my sister, Jenny.' Kate dried her hands and came forward, determinedly friendly and talking too fast. 'Hello, Evelyn, so glad Martin managed to get you here at last. Sorry I wasn't able to greet you before, but as you can see we're knee-deep in turkey stuffing. Is your room okay? I put things out that Pat . . . that perhaps you might need, but if there's anything else you want, just shout.'

'Everything's fine, Mrs Chivers.'

'Oh, call me Kate, please.'

'Can I help with anything?'

'Oh, no, you go and get warm in front of the fire. We're all going to have a drink now you're here.'

36

'Let me fix the drinks,' Tony said. 'What d'you prefer Evelyn, red or white?'

'White is fine.'

'I'd rather have a beer, Dad,' Martin said.

'Help yourself, there's plenty in the fridge. Oh, and Martin,' he added as he departed, 'let your mother tell you about something that's cropped up concerning Uncle Roger.'

On his way to fetch the wine he bumped into his father, on his way to the bathroom. 'Well, I told him.'

'What's that, Pop?'

'Roger. Damn ridiculous, the way he's acting.'

'Yes, well let's keep it to ourselves over Christmas. Jenny, Martin and his girlfriend have arrived, go and say hello to them. They're all in the kitchen.'

'Right. Just use the lav first.' He started towards the stairs.

'Use the one down here. That door.'

Grabbing a bottle of white wine he had left on ice, Tony put his head around the door to the study. Roger was sitting in a chair staring vacantly at the television.

'So, Pop had a go at you, I gather.'

'What else did you expect? He ran true to form.'

'Did you avoid religion?'

'Yes. Just.'

'Good. You okay where you are?'

'Where am I? You tell me.'

'Can I fix you a soft drink?'

'No, thank you. It was a big mistake to come, I see that now.'

'Well, try and make the best of it. I promise I won't make any more cracks.'

As he returned to the kitchen Tony was just in time to hear his father asking Evelyn how long she had known his grandson. 'He's a terror where girls are concerned, you know, chopping and changing. Course, we weren't expecting to see you.'

'Thanks, Grandpa, give me a break, will you?' Martin said. He looked at his sister and rolled his eyes to the ceiling. 'Can I make myself a sandwich?'

'No, wait, you'll spoil your dinner. Go into the living room all of you,' Kate said. 'Go on, everybody leave me to it if you want to eat tonight.'

They duly trooped into the living room. Tony knew what was coming: given a new audience, Pop would move into turbo mode. He and the children would have to close ranks to protect Evelyn. 'It's about time for the seven o'clock news, isn't it?' Jenny said. 'Can we have it on?'

'Yes, sure,' Tony said, 'the control's over there.'

'Nothing worth watching nowadays,' Pop said. 'They want to bring back *The Black and White Minstrel Show, Sunday Night at the Palladium, ITMA.*'

'Wasn't that a radio programme, Pop?' Martin said.

'Course it was,' he replied. 'Kept us going during

the war, that did.' He turned to Evelyn. 'You watch a lot, do you?'

'I like some of the dramas they put on but, no, I'm not glued to it.'

'I saw one the other night, some man whose wife made him frocks that he went shopping in. They've no right to take the licence money for stuff like that. It's the same with the footballers. All that kissing when they score a goal. I blame Harold Wilson, he started it all.'

Brother and sister exchanged knowing glances, their eyes beginning to water as they suppressed their laughter. Winding up Grandpa had long been a favourite ploy. 'Remind me, who did he play for, Pop?' Martin asked.

'Who?'

'Harold Wilson.'

'Play? He didn't play, he was Prime Minister. Don't teach you much at that place, do they?' He lost the thread momentarily then went off at another tangent. 'Of course most people don't study politics like I do.' He looked around the room, eyes glinting, mouth clenched, the tip of his tongue protruding.

'Evelyn studies it, Pop. It's her subject, she lectures in it.'

'Oh, yes?' he said without betraying any interest, for he never relinquished centre stage willingly.

'Can we just watch the headlines for a moment?' Jenny asked as the opening announcements came on the screen. I know why she has to look, Tony thought. With Andy in Belfast the news always held portents for them all. This time, however, the main story concerned a train crash in Italy. The bodies of forty pilgrims on their way to Rome for the Pope's Christmas message had been recovered from the wreckage. 'God certainly took care of them,' he said.

'One of the biggest villains around, the Pope,' his father said, searching for a way back into the limelight.

'Yes, well don't let's get started on religion, Pop.' There was a cutting edge to Tony's voice which had its effect. Although he had long practice in conceding a point with his father rather than argue it, for Jenny's sake he was determined to steer him away from anything that might encroach on the Northern Ireland situation. They watched the remainder of the short news bulletin in silence. Happily, there was no mention of the Troubles, nor did his father pursue any of his former topics; a glass of wine following the sherry and the spitting heat of the fire lulled him and the peace lasted until dinner.

Tony took the opportunity to engage Evelyn in conversation and observe her at close quarters. Since arriving she had changed into a sweater and skirt and he noted she had a trim figure, a little heavy in the bust perhaps, but with good legs. He found himself wondering whether she and Martin had been to bed together and where – her place or Martin's rooms?

Memories of his own early exploits flooded back; since they had both been living with their parents at the time, he and Kate had made do with the back seat of an old Austin 7 and to this day cars still held a certain eroticism for her. Now, as he listened, his writer's imagination placed Evelyn and Martin in a *La Bohème* setting, but that was probably merely fanciful on his part. Oxford had never struck him as another Latin Quarter, but maybe that was just sour grapes because he had never been fortunate enough to have a university education, only envied those who had. He could not pretend that Evelyn was a type he had ever been attracted to, a little too blue-stocking for his taste, but he gave her full marks for easing herself into what could well have been a sticky family situation with good humour. Maybe she would prove to be the stabilising influence he sensed Martin needed. Without seeming too curious, he drew her out, learning that she had first met Martin at a debate when they had both been speaking for the motion. This surprised him, since he had never thought of his son as being capable of speaking about anything other than football and the opposite sex. It just went to show how little he knew about either of his children. He wanted so much for them, too much probably, a happy land where everything stayed bright, and sometimes the realisation that he could not alter anything for them gripped him with cold fingers. The future kept holding out a carrot in front

41

of you, and you plodded after it, but somehow it always eluded you.

His father came to life again as Roger joined them and it jolted Tony that, engrossed with Evelyn, he had completely forgotten that his brother was in the house. Without Vanessa and the two girls he seemed to have no identity.

'Have you rung them?' was his father's immediate question.

'Who's that?'

'Why, Vanessa and the girls.'

'No, not yet,' Roger said, shooting a glance at Evelyn. 'We haven't been introduced, have we? I'm Roger.'

'Sorry, sorry, that's my fault, how rude of me,' Tony said. 'Evelyn, this is my brother.'

Nobody seemed prepared to break the ice with small-talk after that and since Roger wasn't drinking he stood awkwardly in front of the fire, like an actor waiting for a cue who doesn't know what to do with his hands. Despite Pop's blanket condemnation of it, television came to the rescue and they watched part of an old movie, *Miracle on 42nd Street*, until Kate announced that dinner was ready.

During the meal there was one tricky moment when, forgetting the situation, Martin helped Roger to some wine, but he had the good sense not to refuse it, merely leaving it untouched. Somehow the usual Christmas atmosphere was missing; given Roger's moodiness, Martin's gauche efforts to impress and the fact that Evelyn was an outsider to the shorthand codes that all families use in conversation, talk around the table became forced and flat, though Jenny and Kate made a determined effort to keep it going. It was with a feeling of relief that Tony welcomed the arrival of guests as the meal ended. An old-fashioned GP who actually still made house calls as a matter of course, Ted Turner, and his wife, Julie, were their closest, virtually their only, friends in the neighbourhood. Most of the other residents had proved heavy sledding over the twenty years Tony and Kate had lived there and although, at the beginning, they had made valiant efforts to get on their wavelengths, good intentions had invariably floundered. It was a very British failing.

They exchanged gifts with the Turners over coffee and spurred by their arrival, Pop immediately launched into a detailed monologue on his medical history. What is it about doctors, Tony mused, that makes everyone want to get a free diagnosis? You don't open your mouth and ask for a free scaling the moment you meet a dentist, so why are the poor bloody medics singled out? To a lesser extent he suffered himself; button-holed by strangers and forced to reveal his own occupation, he found that most people bored the ass off him by confiding the plot of the novel they would one day write when they had the time.

'This pain I get in my right leg,' his father was saying, 'what brings that on, d'you think?'

'How old are you now, Pop?' Ted said, politely.

'Eighty-two,' Pop replied with obvious pride.

'Sins of your youth catching up with you, I expect.'

The answer pleased Pop. 'Ah, well, yes, I was a bit of a Jack the Lad in those days,' he chuckled.

'Still are, Pop,' Jenny said.

The phone went at that moment and Tony picked it up. It was a girl's voice, asking for Martin, and he recognised it as Patricia's.

'It's for you.'

'Me? Who is it?'

'No idea,' he lied. 'D'you want to take it in my study where it's quiet?'

'Yes, okay.' A premonition changed Martin's face and he avoided looking at anybody as he left the room, acting nonchalant. Tony waited until the other receiver was lifted and then hung up. Looking across the room he caught Kate's eyes and smiled at her. He thought how lucky he was still to find her unpredictable and exciting. 'Do what?' he said. 'Sorry, I was thinking of something else,' as he became aware Ted had been talking to him.

'I wondered how your new book is coming along.'

'Slowly.'

'What's it about this time?'

'The mixture as before, but stirred differently.'

'I loved the last one,' Julie said. 'Very sad, though.

44

And that always puzzles me because you're not a sad person.'

'I keep at him to write a comedy,' Kate said, 'but he won't listen to me.'

'The book of Daddy's I like best is *Wilderness Years*, though come to think of it that has a sad ending too. What is it with you, Daddy? Because Julie's right, you can be hysterical when you choose.'

'Something to do with my genes, I expect. I don't set out to write sad books, it just happens that way.'

'Agatha Christie, now there's a good writer,' his father interjected, seeking a way back into the conversation.

'One of the best, Pop. I wish I had her sales.'

In some curious way talking about his work always embarrassed him and he put this down to the fact that being a writer meant that one was instinctively secretive, living as one did during the creative process in a world that nobody else could enter.

'What d'you think makes a best-seller?' Evelyn asked.

'I wish I knew.'

'A preposterous narrative,' Ted volunteered.

'Not necessarily,' Evelyn said. 'I think it's something more. For some reason people who only read maybe a couple of books a year want to read about power. Power is the buzz word.'

'Not sex?'

'That, too, but it has to be combined with the other.

45

If sex is the *only* thing they want then there's plenty of porn around. Scandal in high places, that's always a good bet, and money, money, money, the power that money brings. It's the average impossible dream, you see, the reason why this country bets millions on the pools every week. Authors like Archer and Jackie Collins understand that and cash in. Soap opera on the page.'

'There you are,' Ted said, 'now you know, so get to it.'

'I've never read any real porn,' Julie said. 'What's it like?'

'Who wants to answer that?' Tony said. 'Don't all rush.'

'I have,' Evelyn said lighting a cigarette, then added, 'Oh, does anybody mind?'

'No, but Ted'll give you a hard time.'

'You have?' Julie returned to the topic.

'Some.'

'I have too,' Kate said.

'When? You've never told me that,' Tony was genuinely surprised.

'At school. We used to pass around *The Awful Disclosures of Maria Monk*.'

'Oh, that old thing. I used to read smuggled copies of Frank Harris and Henry Miller, but they're considered very tame by today's standards.'

'And of course men read *Playboy* strictly for the articles.'

'Ha, ha.'

'Doesn't fascinate me,' Ted said. 'When you've stared at as many naked bodies as I have, you'd rather read *Country Life*.'

'Do I take that as personal?' Julie asked.

'There must be some professional hazards, Ted,' Tony said. 'How many times have you fought off the advances of some rabid female patient?'

'This is a really edifying conversation to have at Christmas,' Kate said shooting a warning look at her husband. 'Don't give away trade secrets, Ted.'

'One thing that's interesting,' Evelyn interjected, 'is that prior to *glasnost*, the Russian literary underground, the refuseniks, used pornography as a political weapon. Of course in any suppressed society sex and religion are the first things to be censored and consequently assume a greater significance.'

'They should bring him back,' Pop said, getting into the discussion for the first time.

'Bring who back, Pop?' Tony said, hoping the answer would not be the public hangman, since capital punishment was one of Pop's favourite topics.

'The whatcha-ma-call-it, Lord Censor chap. What d'you say, Roger?'

'I certainly think that certain moral values have gone out of the window, yes.' The others waited, but he was not to be drawn further.

At that moment Martin returned to the room, his

face slightly waxen, and immediately helped himself to a drink.

'Who was it, darling?' his mother asked out of habit rather than interest.

'Oh, nobody really,' he muttered. 'Somebody from college who wanted a telephone number. I think I might turn in. I expect you're tired too, aren't you?' he added, looking at Evelyn.

'Not really, and I'm having a good time,' she said. 'Unless everybody else is ready?' His abruptness had embarrassed her.

'Suit yourself. I'll say good-night then.' He kissed his mother and Julie, then left the room.

'My brother the social charmer,' Jenny said, as everybody exchanged glances.

'We ought to be getting on our way, too,' Julie said. 'My doctor friend here is on call tomorrow, believe it or not. The trains aren't running, but doubtless he will be. Thanks for our lovely presents, Kate dear.'

'Thank you for yours.'

Good-nights were exchanged all round and Tony went with them to the door. 'With Vanessa and the children not here it seems funny not to be doing the stockings,' Kate said, as she began to gather up the glasses and coffee cups. 'Still, I expect they'll be having a good time where they are.'

'I'm sure they will,' Roger said.

'Is everybody going to bed?' Pop asked. 'Nobody wants to have a game of whist or something?'

'Not tonight, Pop. I think we're all whacked, I know I am.'

'We always play whist at Christmas.'

'Well, perhaps tomorrow. Have you got everything you need, Evelyn?'

'Yes, thank you. And thank you for a lovely dinner. It's a long time since I had a family Christmas, I'd forgotten what it's like.'

Three

They lay in bed listening to the snow shifting on the roof and every so often they heard a whole section fall off.

'Must be thawing,' Tony said.

'Oh, I hope not. I want it to be a white Christmas.'

'Well, we've survived round one without a knock-down . . . but keep your gum-shield in. I still can't get over Roger, can you?'

'Vanessa's the one I feel sorry for. Soon as I get a chance I must ring her. Aren't families extraordinary?'

'Don't suppose ours is all that extraordinary. Remember Keith and Alison, what they went through last year? Their father was arrested as a cross-dresser performing oral sex in a lay-by on the M4.'

'Yes, wasn't that awful.'

'At least Pop hasn't treated us to that . . . What did you make of Evelyn?'

'Different from what I was expecting. You never know with Martin.'

'I think she's good news. Least you can have an intelligent conversation. Who was that one last year? Melissa. All her brains were in her tits.'

'Trust you to remember those.'

'Difficult to forget them. She was almost deformed. No, I must say I've taken to Evelyn, and the fact that she's mature might be quite a good thing for Martin. He could do with a little maturity.'

'I don't know if I'm going to get to sleep tonight,' Kate said, 'I've got so much on my mind. I may have to take a pill. No, I'd better not otherwise I'll be a zombie in the morning, and I must get up early and put the turkey in. I never know how long to give the blessed things, every cook-book says something different.'

'You know who it was that rang him? Patricia. I'm sure I recognised her voice. I bet that's why he came back into the room looking like Marley's ghost and went straight to bed. I wonder what that was about? . . . Listen!' he said suddenly.

'What?'

'Thought I heard something.'

'Is the alarm on?'

'Yes. Not that. I've got one ear cocked for that bloody boiler.'

They both listened. 'No, just the snow I think.'

'You sure it wasn't them?'

'Who?'

'Martin and her.'

'No, it was a thump.'

'Could be them . . . D'you think they do it?'

'Probably.'

'But he's only just met her.'

'Well, we didn't waste much time, if you recall.'

'That was different.'

'Was it? Why?'

'Well, it was safer then,' Kate said. 'D'you think they're doing it now?'

'Darling, how do I know? What do you want me to do, go and listen at the door?'

'I think you should get him on his own and talk to him tomorrow. Warn him not to get too involved.' She was like every mother, trying to fathom the hidden life of a son who had left her. 'I know those sort of women. Probably had a dozen affairs. For all we know she may be married. Did you find anything out when you talked to her?'

'No.'

'Nothing?'

'Well, I didn't ask her those sort of questions.'

Kate was silent for a few moments, then said: 'It isn't normal to be sleeping with a woman twice his age.'

'Katy,' he said, 'remember the old saying – "in the dark all cats are grey". If you're right, presumably she knows her way around.'

'Do you think she's attractive?'

'She has a certain something, yes.'

'What?'

'What?'

'Yes.' Kate sat up in bed and turned to him. 'What d'you find attractive about her?'

'I don't.'

'You just said.'

'I was merely looking at it from Martin's point of view, that's all.'

'But what "something" has she got?'

'For me, nothing, but I guess she turns him on. Or maybe she doesn't, maybe they just hold hands and discuss politics, who knows? Just be grateful he's not into drugs. Look, take that sleeping pill, and stop worrying.'

'I can't help worrying. Everything worries me.'

They were embarked on a collision course they had travelled before, first when Jenny was going through the process of natural selection and now with Martin. 'Sweetheart,' he said soothingly, 'Martin has to live his own life. It never works to interfere. You weren't that keen on Andy at one time, now you think he's the cat's whiskers. No one Martin's age quite knows what he's doing. I didn't. It's simply biological. Remember how we carried on.'

'That was different,' she said again.

'What was so different about it?'

'It just was,' Kate replied, refusing to be diverted

from her reasoning. 'We were more or less the same age when we got together.'

'You're missing the point.'

'All I mean is, we knew we were going to get married.'

'Did we?'

'Well, yes, of course we did.'

'How soon they forget. All I was interested in was getting you in the sack as often as possible. Biological. I mooned about with a permanent erection.' He put his arm around her. 'We weren't any different, we were just lucky.'

'You're probably right. You usually are. I guess I'm worrying unnecessarily. I don't know what it is, but every little thing throws me these days, and this Christmas has started all wrong.'

Tony kissed the nape of her neck.

'I can't right now,' she said. 'I must get to sleep.'

'It might send you to sleep. My tried and tested remedy.' He suddenly leapt out of bed.

'Now, what is it?'

'Wait. I nearly forgot.' He rummaged at the bottom of his wardrobe and produced a gift-wrapped parcel. 'Open your present from me now.'

'But it's not Christmas morning yet.'

'Yes it is, it's gone midnight. Open it.'

'Why?'

'You'll see. Come on, you won't have time to appreciate it in the morning when you're rushing around.'

She opened the parcel carefully, and took out a white, lawn nightdress.

'Like it?'

'Oh, it's ravishing.'

'Try it on.'

'Now?'

'Yes, now. That's what it's for.'

She got out of bed and removed her pyjamas, then slipped the gift over her head.

'It looks great on you. Have a look at yourself.' She went to the mirror. 'Very sexy.' He went behind her while she was admiring it and put his hands around her, cupping her breasts.

'Um . . . ' Kate said, admiring herself. 'You're right, it is sexy . . . ' She turned round and kissed him. 'You talked me into it.'

Four

Feeling neither crisp nor even Tony woke to Christmas morning from a disturbing and vaguely erotic dream about his old schoolteacher. They had been sharing a Jacuzzi but, curiously, although he had been naked, Miss Anderson of blessed memory had been in a suspender belt and smoking a cigar. What the hell could that mean? Slowly emerging into the real world, he turned over in bed and reached for Kate, but she was not there. He groped for his wristwatch and saw that the time was only just past seven. Pale sunlight, made more intense by being reflected off the snow, glinted on the wall opposite. Why Miss Anderson? he thought. It must be all of thirty years since I sat in the classroom trying to get a glimpse of her legs from under her desk. She had been the sixth form's pin-up, the only begetter of a thousand adolescent fantasies and eventually justifying those fantasies when she was caught *in flagrante delicto* with

Pip Harrison, the school captain, in the cricket pavilion. But smoking a cigar! he thought, carrying the image with him into the bathroom, that was clearly a potent sexual signal sending only one suggestive message. Bleary, his greying hair looking like one of those mysterious circles that appear in corn fields, he studied the night's ravages in the mirror. Dear Miss Anderson, he thought, where are you now? Where are any of us?

Snatches of the dream stayed with him as he shaved and he found himself dredging up other memories from the past: Cohen, the boy who sat in front of him, ablaze with acne; Mathews, his best friend who was killed on a motorcycle the first day he had it; and Violet Smith, the agony and the ecstasy of his last term, who had never given him the time of day. The mood locked in, staying with him while he dressed and he bemoaned the years the locusts had eaten. Miss Anderson in a Jacuzzi, he thought. Dream on.

Kate and Jenny were already hard at work in the kitchen.

'Happy Christmas,' he said and kissed them. 'Any coffee on?'

'Over there.'

'I had the strangest dream,' he began, but then decided not to pursue it. One's own dreams meant nothing to other people and in any case he suddenly felt protective about the memory of Miss Anderson.

'When you've come to,' Kate said, 'do the fires, will you? Oh, and Emily's left something disgusting on the mat which Jenny and I can't face.'

'What makes you think I can face it?'

'Because she's your cat.'

'Since when?'

He took his coffee and examined the evidence. It appeared to be the rear end of a squirrel. Putting on kitchen gloves he averted his face and picked it up to take outside. The air was squeaky clear, taking his breath away at first gulp, and he crunched his way to the dustbins then stood listening to that peculiar silence that always envelops the world on Christmas Day – the usual steady rumble of traffic from the distant motorway was absent and it seemed as though overnight the entire population had been evacuated. As he stood savouring his coffee an icicle detached itself from the roof of the shed, landing upright in the snow like a dagger. Coloured lights burned on the tree outside the house opposite and he remembered a time when his belief in the mystique of the nativity had been absolute. Where had that gone, too? He suddenly became conscious that he had wandered outside in his slippers and that they were now sodden. Emily appeared as he turned to go inside, padding disdainfully across the snow. She lifted and shook her paws after every few steps with a fixed expression on her face.

'You murderer,' Tony said to her, 'don't you know

this is the season of peace on earth and goodwill towards all squirrels?'

Master of the sudden dash, Emily sped ahead of him and slid inside the kitchen before he could close the door.

'The cat's in,' he shouted.

'Well, find her and sling her out. If she so much as looks at any of this food her days are numbered,' Kate replied.

Removing his damp slippers, Tony went through the house searching for the animal without success, then lost interest and began the task of re-laying the fires. They were still using wood blown down in the last great storm, mostly silver birch that he had planted the year they moved in. He used dry fir cones to start the one in the living room, squatting in front of it, mesmerised, until the flames took hold. His knee joints cracked as he straightened to find a dishevelled Martin hovering in the doorway.

'Morning, old sport,' Tony said. 'Merry Christmas.'

'Yes. Merry Christmas, Dad.'

'How goes it? Sleep well?'

'So-so. Where is everybody?'

'Well, your mother and Jenny left to catch the early plane to Paris, your grandfather and Roger are out playing ice hockey . . . where d'you think everybody is? Go into the kitchen and frighten them.'

The attempt at humour produced nothing but a blank expression.

'Can I talk to you, Dad?'

'Sure,' Tony said, although his parental radar had already detected a Scud missile of doom heading his way.

Martin began slowly, shifting from side to side in the doorway. His old dressing gown with its braided cord and torn pockets made him look much younger than his twenty years.

'The thing is, I might have got myself into a sort of situation.'

'Uh, huh. What kind of situation? Money?'

'No, not money . . . well, maybe money . . . You remember Patricia?'

'Very well. D'you want to come in and close the door?'

Martin did as suggested. 'She phoned last night,' he began again, then faltered.

'Yes, I had an idea that might have been her.'

'It's about Patricia.'

'So you said. I thought that was all over?'

'Well, it was, but the reason she rang was to tell me she might be in trouble.'

Tony looked back at the fire and waited, but when Martin didn't elaborate he said: 'What sort of trouble?'

'Well, she's not sure and it could be, you know, nothing at all to worry about, she could have got her dates mixed up . . . but . . . well, she's missed two of her . . . it's been two months since she had one.'

'Uh, huh. The curse, you mean?'

'Yes.' A certain relief flooded into his face now that the operative word had finally been spoken. 'She doesn't usually, you see, that's why she's worried.'

'And she wanted you to know?'

'Yes.'

'For reasons we can take as read, yes?' Martin nodded. 'Okay. Well, don't panic. It could be a false alarm.'

'Could it?'

'Oh, yes, happens all the time. Funny creatures, women. Their bodies work in mysterious ways. But let me ask you something. The precautions you take . . . I assume, I hope, you *do* take precautions, don't you? . . . Could they, did they . . . ' It was Tony's turn to search for the right words. 'Can you remember an occasion when you thought they might not have done what they're supposed to?'

'Er . . . maybe, yes, probably.'

'Well, which is it?'

'Yes.'

'What d'you use, the Pill or condoms?'

'Condoms.'

'In my day we called them french letters. You could only buy them at the hairdressers. After you'd had a basin cut the barber would whisper, ''Anything else, sir?'' It was all very discreet,' Tony said, trying to ease the situation, but Martin's expression did not change. Tony tried again: 'So you think you might have had a dud, do you?'

61

'Well, about the time when it could have happened, we did feel one of them wasn't a hundred per cent.'

I've got to be equal to this situation, Tony thought. Calm, not scare him unnecessarily, but on the other hand treat it seriously, be lucid, understanding, give the right advice. 'You tested it, did you? Afterwards?'

Martin nodded, the intimacy suddenly too much.

'Well, then, we have to accept that it could be a possibility. Pat obviously thinks the worst. Was she in a state?'

'Scared shitless,' Martin blurted. 'See, her parents are Catholics.'

'Has she told them?'

'God, no. That's the last thing she wants to do.'

'So what was she asking you to do?'

'She wasn't. She was just crying.'

'Tell me one thing, because it's important – why did you split up? D'you want a cigarette?'

'Yes, thanks.' Tony gave him a light and lit one himself. Oh, God, he thought, now I'm bonding.

'It was all a bit stupid really,' his tongue loosened by the shared vice. 'I happened to go out with Evelyn a couple of times, just social, nothing heavy, and didn't tell Pat, but she found out and we had a big row.'

'Happens. Are you still fond of her?'

'I don't know. Yes, I suppose so.'

'How fond?'

'Quite a lot.'

'Does Evelyn know any of this?'

'No, I haven't said anything.'

'Well, in the circumstances, being wise after the event, it might have been better if you'd made it up and brought Pat here as planned. Your mother's so much better at these things than I am.'

'Yes, I see that now. But I was upset too. Will you tell Mummy?'

'D'you want me to?'

'Rather you than me.'

At that moment they heard Roger's voice in the hallway. 'Okay, leave it with me for the time being,' Tony said. 'Let me think about it and we'll talk later. Hang in there.'

Roger came in. 'Oh, there you are. Morning. Morning, Martin, compliments of the season.'

Martin muttered a return greeting and made good his escape.

Roger said: 'I thought I should tell you the loo in my bathroom seems to have frozen solid during the night.'

'Well, of course it has,' Tony said savagely. 'They wanted to use this house for *Nightmare on Elm Street*. Okay, I'll deal with it. You haven't seen the cat, have you?'

'No, why would I have seen the cat?'

'Just asking. There's coffee in the kitchen if you want some. Did you try peeing on the frozen loo.'

'Certainly not. Too much consideration for others.'

'Well, use the downstairs one.' He took a last look at the fire to make sure it was well alight, put the guard in place, then followed his brother into the kitchen. 'Is there a kettle on?' he asked Kate. 'I need some hot water.'

'The boiler hasn't gone off, has it?'

'No, this is something else. Don't ask what.'

'Morning, Roger dear,' Kate said. 'Happy Christmas. Martin, don't stand just there, take your breakfast into the other room. Let me look at you. You look peaky, you're not coming down with flu, are you?'

'No, mother, I'm fine. Just my morning look.'

Tony took a kettle of boiling water upstairs to do battle with the loo and was just in time to stop an emerging Evelyn from using it.

'Slight disaster in that one, Evelyn. Go into our bathroom, the door over there. Hope you were warm enough, were you?'

'I went out, bang.'

'Well, good. Merry Christmas.'

'And to you.'

Her silk dressing gown clung to her form, revealing more than it concealed and as he watched her disappear Tony thought, I can quite see the attraction she has for Martin, potential father though he may be. Entering the offending loo he discovered that somebody had left the window open. He poured the kettle of hot water on the ice, then closed the seat, stood on it and fastened the window. The chewed end of a cheroot, the type his father smoked, rested on the sill and once again the delectable Miss Anderson, she of the endless long legs, swam before his eyes. Why was life such a bitch?

Before going downstairs he looked into his father's room, finding him still in bed with Emily curled on the counterpane.

'Oh, that's where she is! Been looking all over for her. Come on you, out!' He gathered her up, but Emily clung to the counterpane with extended claws like a mountaineer on the Eiger. 'Everything okay, Pop? Have a good night?'

'Very fair. Everybody else up?'

'Yes. But take your time, no hurry. Oh, and be careful using the loo, I've just been trying to unfreeze it.'

'Frozen, is it?' Disasters always roused his father. 'Yes, well it would be given this weather. Didn't you lag the pipes?'

'Somebody left the window open.'

'That would do it,' his father agreed. He had his teeth out and his speech was sibilant. 'That would do it for certain. No papers, I suppose?'

'No, they don't publish today.'

'Pity, pity. What's it like outside?'

'Nice and bright.' Tony opened the curtains with his free hand while keeping a firm hold on the struggling cat.

'Is Roger going to church this morning? If so, I'll go with him. Always like to go once a year.'

'I'm not sure, I'll ask him,' Tony said as he left to eject the disgruntled Emily out of the front door. He checked the fires again, then, as he threw another log on, the tree lights failed. He went to the tree and shook it. The angel sagged sideways. Panicked, he stood on a chair and was attempting to repair the damage when Kate caught him in the act.

'What're you doing?'

'What does it look like I'm doing? The tree must have shifted during the night.'

'How? Nobody was in here.'

'Maybe poltergeists.'

'And what's happened to the lights again? I thought you were going to get Roger to fix them?'

'I will, I will. So far, and the day is still young, all I've done is disposed of a squirrel carcass, lit the fires, unfrozen a loo, found the missing cat and given advice to the lovelorn.'

'What's that mean?' Kate said, latching on to his last remark.

'It'll keep.'

'No, tell me.'

'I don't want you getting all upset.'

'Tony . . . tell me.'

'Oh, Martin is a bit frayed. That call he had last night was from his ex, who may be about to make us grandparents.'

'Oh, God!'

'See. I didn't want to tell you until later.'

'How far along is she?'

'Two months according to your son.'

'Suddenly he's just my son?'

'*Our* son then. It'll probably prove to be a false alarm.'

'She won't turn up here, will she?'

'The way things are going, who knows? But I doubt it. Don't get into another state.'

'Easy for you to say that. Well, I'm not going to think about it. I just can't at the moment. This room needs tidying before Jenny's friends get here. I want the place to look nice.'

'I'll do it, you get on with what you've got to do.'

'Nobody thinks of me,' Kate said, plumping cushions. 'You realise we'll have three complete strangers in the house?'

'It's understandable, darling. I guess she misses Andy and wanted some friends of her own age.'

'I miss Andy but that doesn't mean we hang out a sign like Barnardo's – "Nobody in need refused admission." What did you say to Martin?'

'Nothing much.'

'You must have said something.'

'I tried to play it down.'

'You can't play babies down. If they're there, they're there. Poor girl, she must be worried silly. Oh, God, our children. Martin can't become a father at his age, he's still at university.'

'It happens.'

'Well, it's not going to happen to him. You must make them see sense.'

'Darling, I can't do anything today, can I? The trains aren't even running, so I doubt whether abortion clinics are open for business.'

'Don't shout and don't turn nasty.'

'All right, okay, I didn't mean to shout. I'll deal with it as soon as we get today over.'

'Promise. God, I must time the bloody turkey. Jenny and I could only just get it into that stupid oven. I shouldn't have bought such a big one, but I wasn't to know half of them weren't coming. It's meant to be in for five hours, so remind me just before one. Have you put out the glasses and done the drinks?'

'No, but I will. Darling, we have to try and enjoy it otherwise we'll both go mad. Smile. Come on, smile, it'll all sort itself out.'

'I wish I had your optimism.'

'It isn't optimism, its fatalism. Now calm down and wish me a Happy Christmas.' They kissed and the tree lights came on. 'There, you see! Uri Geller step aside. After lunch I might bend some spoons. Listen, we'll survive this, go and put a face on and I'll make some fresh coffee.'

'No, I can't, I haven't seen to Pop yet, you know he has to have a cooked breakfast.'

'I'll take care of that.'

'Can you? He has two boiled eggs, toast and tea. You sure you can manage?'

'You know me. Delia Smith with balls. Go on.'

He pottered to the kitchen again where Jenny was clearing up the debris. 'Who are these friends of yours who are coming?'

'Harvey and Bill.'

Since Andy was away so often and she wasn't too keen on Army accommodation Jenny had taken a small flat and a secretarial job in the London office of an American computer firm.

'You'll like them, they're good news.'

'I need good news. What do they do?'

'Harvey's the phantom of the computer and Bill does public relations. You don't mind, do you?'

'No, course not.' He dropped two eggs into a saucepan of water and immediately both shells cracked. Strings of white snaked from the eggs and then became a froth which overflowed the sides of the pan. Tony stared at the mess in horror.

'Why have they done that?'

Jenny looked and took the pan off the flame. 'Let me do them, you do the toast. You should have started them in cold water.'

'Stupid bloody things. They're as stupid as the hens that lay them. I've never liked hens. They peck each other's bottoms, which can't be what nature intended. Remember when I tried to keep them – one of my many schemes to get rich – and the eggs worked out at seven and six each? Now, that's funny . . . '

'What is?'

69

'I said the price in old money.'

'You used to do good chicken impersonations for us, though, Daddy.'

'I still can.' Thrilled that she recalled such idiocies, he crouched and worked his arms like wings, then began to produce low broody clucks which built to a squawking crescendo as he laid an imaginary egg.

'I named them all,' Jenny said, laughing with him. 'What about the one I called Jesus? I cried when he – she – had to be killed. I still feel a bit squeamish whenever I have chicken. Daddy, since I've literally saved your bacon and eggs, can I open my presents?'

'Sure, soon as everybody's down. What did you think of Evelyn?'

'Seems fine. It won't last of course. She's too street-wise for Martin.'

'And too old?'

'Oh, that doesn't come into it. Not nowadays, anything goes.'

'I'm glad you and Martin get on better now. You do, don't you?'

'Yes, in small doses. He's all right, a bit of a dickhead.'

Tony suddenly lunged as a piece of blackened toast shot out of the toaster like Challenger being launched, but failed to catch it.

'Daddy, let me do the whole thing.'

'Kitchens aren't my natural habitat. Still I can't be a genius at everything.'

'Patricia's yesterday's news presumably?' Jenny said as she put two new pieces of bread under the grill.

'I think she's in holding pattern. How much longer has Andy got over there?'

'They're meant to be relieving his lot next month.'

'Then what?'

'He doesn't know. There was a rumour about Bosnia, which I'm praying doesn't happen. Isn't the world in a mess?'

'Ghastly. But you're happy. You are happy, aren't you?'

'Of course, why d'you ask?'

'No particular reason.'

'It's difficult being separated, that's the only thing.'

'Why don't you come back here for a while?'

'Daddy, we've got a place of our own now. It won't last for ever, I just have to sweat it out.'

Looking at her, he felt a consuming nostalgia for times past, choosing to forget the period when she, like Martin now, had driven them mad – dressing like a truck driver and introducing a series of callow swains into the household. It was only since her marriage that he had felt relaxed with her. Before there had always been a latent tension, mainly, he supposed, because she and Kate had been rivals for his affections and he had avoided taking sides which, in turn, had led to arguments. Now he had no need to conceal the special kind of love, unlike any other, he had always felt for her. He had been surprised to find that he harboured no resentment towards Andy; the fact that she often said 'He's so like you, Daddy, in many ways' gratified him. When did the metamorphosis from argumentative teenager to assured adult happen? he wondered, stepping out of her way as she busied herself fixing the breakfast tray. I'm her father, why is she a mystery? How would I set about describing her character in a novel? I could find the words to conjure up her physical qualities – the overlarge mouth she inherited from Kate and which gives her such an infectious smile, the small bust which, again like Kate's, will never sag, the maddening way she constantly brushes the fringe out of her eyes – all that would be easy enough, but what of her night thoughts?

'Why are you looking at me like that?' Jenny said.

'How was I looking?'

'Sort of confused.'

'I'm always confused,' he said, 'that's nothing new.'

'Everything's all right, isn't it?'

'Couldn't be better.'

She finished preparing her grandfather's tray. 'I'll take this up to him, be nice for him to have it in bed, and it saves messing up the dining room.'

'He doesn't change, does he?'

'Why should he?'

'No, I suppose you're right. I expect I'll be a cantankerous old sod when I'm his age.'

'What have you got Mummy? Tell me, I won't let on.'

'Nothing.'

'Nothing!? I don't believe you.'

He pulled a face at her. 'Just kidding. I gave it to her last night, if you'll pardon the expression.' Jenny raised an eyebrow which he acknowledged with a wink.

Taking the tray upstairs she found her grandfather sitting on the edge of the bed staring out of the window and for a second she thought he wasn't well. 'I've brought your breakfast, Pop. Sorry it took so long.'

'That's good of you, love.'

As he took the tray from her she noticed how covered in age-spots his hands were and the old-fashioned wrist watch with the worn leather strap. She was suddenly ashamed of the irritation she had sometimes felt with him. Sitting there in flannel pyjamas that had seen better days, he had a frailty about him that wasn't normally apparent for, whatever else, he always kept himself spruce when clothed. Now the white stubble on his cheeks caught the light, reminding her of a tramp who had once frightened her as a child, and she bent and kissed his cheek.

'I hope these are done enough for you. When you're ready we're going to open the presents.'

'I've got mine,' he said. 'In that carrier bag over there.'

'Gosh! What's in it? You always spoil us.'

'That's what Christmas is for, love. Then Roger and I are going to the church service.'

'Are you?' She tried to keep a note of doubt out of her voice.

'Somebody left the window open and of course it froze up.' The non-sequitur flummoxed her.

'Sorry, Pop?'

'The lavatory out there.'

'I'll take a look,' As she left the room she glimpsed Martin and Evelyn talking earnestly on the landing, but the moment she appeared Martin steered Evelyn into her bedroom and closed the door. Downstairs her father was carrying in more logs.

'Pop says he and Roger are going to church together, d'you think that's on?'

'Not unless he takes him to the mosque.'

'Oh, Daddy, you are terrible, you told me not to joke. I hope everybody hurries up, I want to open the presents. I miss not having a stocking at the end of my bed.'

'Stocking? It was always a pillow case.'

Jenny examined the tags under the tree. 'This one's from you. What is it? Give me a clue.'

'No way.'

'I bet you didn't wrap them.'

'I bet I didn't even buy them.'

'Oh, Daddy, I do think you're funny.'

She sat on her haunches looking up at him, then, as

74

the phone rang, her expression changed and she scrambled to answer it first. He knew then that, whatever she felt for him, now there was somebody else in her life, funnier than he could ever be. The excitement in her face died. 'Oh, hello Vanessa, how are you all? I expect the children are excited, did they wake you up early? . . . Yes, I know she wants to speak to you, I'll get her.'

She left the receiver off the hook and went to the foot of the stairs. 'Mummy, it's Vanessa. Say when you've got it and I'll hang up.'

'I expect he'll ring as soon as he can,' Tony said.

'Yes. Sometimes they're a long way from a phone.'

Deflated, the previous mood shattered, she seemed much younger suddenly.

Five

It was another half an hour before the whole family was rounded up and assembled in the living room for the present ritual to begin. It had always been understood that Pop was allowed to give his gifts first. This year they were a novelty corkscrew for Roger (innocently quite the wrong choice), two Disney videos for Martin that he would have preferred when much younger, a Swiss Army knife for Jenny that required a guided tour, and, the *pièce de resistance*, for Kate and Tony a frightening ceramic figure of a man fishing, perched on multi-coloured rocks, complete with rod, line and dangling fish which immediately dropped off. All crudely bound like mummies with yards of Scotch tape.

'Oh, thank you, Pop, just what we wanted,' Kate said, as the children looked away. 'It's lovely, isn't it, darling?'

'Fantastic,' Tony said.

'Took me a time to find that,' his father said, basking in the moment. 'The man in the shop said you won't find another piece like that in a hurry. They're limited. Got his name on the bottom.'

It also still had the price on the bottom. 'So it has,' Kate enthused. 'It's very special, and I'm sure very expensive, you shouldn't have.'

'Wait a minute, wait a minute. You thought I'd forgotten something, didn't you, love?' He handed Kate a last parcel from out of his bag.

'Let me guess,' she said. In a misguided moment she had once said she liked pickled cucumbers and ever since he had relentlessly produced a jar at Christmas. Tearing the wrapping she revealed another addition to the collection she kept hidden in the pantry. 'You remembered!' she exclaimed.

'Your favourites,' Martin said wickedly, while Evelyn, not being in on the family joke, looked perplexed.

The privileges of age having been exercised, then it was the turn of everybody else as the pile of gifts under the tree was distributed.

'Think how many rain forests are demolished every year for this lot,' Tony said as the discarded wrapping paper was strewn around.

'Well, things have to be wrapped.'

'Why, we just tear it off?'

'I don't, I take mine off carefully,' Jenny said.

'You still throw it away.'

Jenny had been given an expensive silk shirt from her parents, together with a belt, both of which produced squeals of delight. Women and clothes, Tony thought, as his daughter rushed upstairs to try on the shirt, most of them would rather have clothes than a meal.

Evelyn, the outsider to it all, now hesitantly produced her own gifts. Not knowing anybody except Martin, she had chosen the safe option of book tokens, with the exception of Tony to whom she gave a leather-bound copy of Connolly's *The Unquiet Grave*.

'I hope you haven't got it already.'

'No, brilliant. I used to have a copy of the original Horizon edition, but it eventually fell to pieces. I'm thrilled. Look, I got lucky.' He held it up for the others to see.

'What's that about then?' Pop asked.

'It's a sort of modern classic,' Tony explained.

'Oh, like Dickens, is it? Good story?'

'More an autobiography.'

His father frowned. 'Still, I expect you'll enjoy it. Prefer a good story myself.'

'This is yours from us, Pop,' Kate jumped in, handing him a large parcel. 'And if it doesn't fit I'll change it.' The wrapping off, it proved to be a thick towelling dressing gown which, since he had never had one, seemed to baffle the old man for a moment. 'Very nice, love, very nice. You wear this indoors, do you?'

'When you've had your bath.'

'Ah, yes, I see. Come in handy, that will.'

'Let me see how it looks, put it on now.'

He levered himself out of his chair and Kate dressed him in the robe and tied the cord around his portly stomach.

'There! Suits you. You look very dashing. Doesn't he look dashing?'

He sat down again, still wearing it, well pleased.

Martin had given all three women perfume and ties to the men – 'You know me, always inspired' – while Roger's gifts were, as usual, blatantly expensive, as though he needed to draw attention to the difference between his own and Tony's fortunes. When it was his turn to receive, Kate and Tony exchanged uneasy glances as he unwrapped the second-hand sweater.

'Not too garish, is it?' Kate asked, fingers crossed behind her back.

'No, no. Perhaps not the sort I'd buy for myself, but it's very fetching.'

They breathed again, though there was a moment of angst when Martin commented, 'It's not unlike one you had, Dad,' before a laser-look from his mother silenced him from elaborating further.

Jenny returned to parade her new shirt. 'What d'you think, Mummy? And I've seen the greatest pair of trousers and waistcoat in Harrods to go with it when I get my next money. I just love it.' She turned to show her grandfather. 'Don't you look smart, too,

Pop. Oh, sorry, here Daddy, this is from Andy and me.' She kissed him, 'I hope to God it's right. I haven't got a clue, but Harvey chose it, so blame him if it's wrong.'

'No, indeed, it isn't wrong.' He held up the box for all to see. 'DOS 6! You're brilliant, I'd been going to treat myself to this.'

'What is it?' Pop asked.

'Something for his computer, I think,' Kate said.

'The latest update.'

'Mummy, where's yours to Daddy?'

'Those there.' They were duly unwrapped – the pullover he already knew about, a Waterman pen identical to the one she had given him two Christmases ago which he tactfully omitted to point out, and a year's subscription to *PC World*. All that remained under the tree were the packages intended for Vanessa and the children.

'You'll take those with you, won't you?' Kate said pointedly.

'Yes, of course,' Roger said.

'And mine,' his father said. 'Don't forget mine.'

'She phoned a little while back. I expect you'll ring the girls before lunch,' Kate added with unmistakable emphasis.

'Yes, I intend to.'

Sensing an atmosphere developing, Jenny said, 'Get your Polaroid, Daddy, and take some pictures. I want to send one to Andy.'

They posed for the photos, Roger stiffly and Pop, bulky in his gift, grinning maniacally. Everybody agreed that they had all been more than lucky, as always. The debris of pleasures was scattered around the floor and not for the first time Tony thought how quickly it was all over: the weeks of preparation disappeared like a Chinese meal which appeared to fill you, but soon afterwards left you feeling empty.

'About time for church,' his father said. 'Are you ready, Roger?'

'What's that, Pop?'

'Church. We ought to be going.'

'I don't think I will this morning, if you don't mind,' Roger said. 'I've got a bit of a headache.'

'Oh.' The old man's disappointment could be felt.

'I'll go with you, Pop,' Jenny said quickly. 'Let me just change out of this and put on something warmer.'

'Yes, wrap up,' her mother said.

When they had left Tony rounded on his brother. 'You could have made the effort, wouldn't have hurt you to go with him.'

'Well, doesn't matter, Jenny's gone,' Kate said, conscious of Evelyn. She busied herself clearing up the discarded paper. 'Let's all have a drink and christen the mince pies. Put some Christmas music on.'

'Can I help?' Evelyn asked, going with her while Martin wandered off elsewhere.

'You're such a prick sometimes,' Tony said when he and Roger were alone. 'You don't see the old man that often, and what would it have been? – an hour out of your life.'

'I can't be hypocritical.'

'Oh, come off it. Why don't you go back on the booze? It made you vaguely human. And I'm not trying to pick a fight, I just want this to be a pleasant day with no dramas.'

'Perhaps it'd have been better if I hadn't come.'

'I didn't say that and I'm not making any judgements. If you've found Mohammed, I'm pleased for you, believe me, but give some thought to others. If you're not going to church, at least ring Vanessa and the kids.'

'Dad,' Martin said, returning to the room, 'switch on the television, there's something we ought to see.'

'Not at the moment, Martin. I'm talking to Roger.'

'It's about Northern Ireland.'

Tony stopped. 'What about it?'

'I don't know. There's a news flash coming up.'

Tony grabbed the remote control and flicked it. 'Which channel?'

'BBC 1.'

They waited anxiously as the image came into focus, missing the first few words, but caught the news reader saying: '. . . *a British armoured vehicle carrying out a routine border patrol came under attack early this morning, suffering severe damage from a remote-controlled bomb. It is not yet known whether there were any fatal casualties. The incident breaks the thirty-six-hour ceasefire announced by the IRA. Further details will be given in our later bulletins. And now we return you to the service from Salisbury Cathedral.'*

Tony switched the set off.

'Oh, Lord,' Roger said. 'It never ends.'

Martin said, 'D'you think we ought to tell Jenny when she gets back?'

'No, wait and see,' his father cautioned. 'It isn't necessarily anything to do with Andy's troop. When's the next news?'

'One o'clock, isn't it?'

'Andy might have rung by then.'

All three looked at each other. 'Those bloody people,' Roger said. 'They don't even care what day it is. It's a war, of course, and the sooner we realise that the better. Either that or pull out. It's not worth another soldier's life.'

'I suppose there'd be a blood bath if we did.'

'There's been a blood bath for the past twenty-five years, so what's the difference?'

'I don't know what Jenny'd do if anything happened to Andy.' Tony shot a warning look at Martin as Kate and Evelyn returned with a plate of hot mince pies.

'Have you opened the champagne, darling?'

'No, just about to.' But before he could uncork the

bottle they saw a car draw up outside and two young men get out.

'Oh, God, that'll be Jenny's friends, and she isn't here. If only you'd gone to church with him, Roger. You let them in, darling, and explain. What are their names?'

'Harvey and Bill,' Tony said as he went to the front door.

'Is it okay to leave our car parked here, sir?' one of the young men shouted.

'Oh, sure, nobody's going out.' It was a long time since he'd been called 'sir'. 'Be careful, the path's very slippery. So glad you found your way.'

'Yeah, so are we. Jenny's directions weren't the greatest. You're her father, sir, I take it?'

'For my sins.'

'Good to meet you, sir. I'm Harvey, and this here is Bill.'

'And I'm Tony, please.'

The two Americans were both in their late twenties, clean-cut, with neat hair reminding him of the way young executives were portrayed in films: casually elegant in sports jackets, sharp-looking jeans, button-down Oxford shirts and crew-neck sweaters. Shaking hands he noticed the one called Bill had one ear pierced with a plain gold ring. Both were carrying elaborately wrapped gifts.

'Where did you have to come from?'

'London – Kensington – via Slough, is it?' He

pronounced it 'Sluff' and Tony let it go uncorrected. 'God knows where we went, but people we asked were very helpful.'

'I'm sorry Jenny isn't here to welcome you. She's gone to church with her grandfather, but they'll be back shortly. But you timed it well, I was just about to open the champagne, so come on in and meet the others.'

The introductions accomplished, Harvey proffered his package to Kate. 'A little Christmas something.'

'How exciting. I recognise the paper.' She opened it. Inside was a small porcelain box from Tiffany. 'You are kind, thank you so much. Look what I've got, Tony.'

Bill held out his package to Tony. 'No prizes for guessing what this is,' he said.

Tony stopped wrestling with the champagne cork and shook his gift. 'Feels suspiciously like something liquid.' He tore the wrapping to reveal a boxed bottle of single malt. 'My favourite, how did you know?'

'I think your daughter had a hand in it.'

'We'll sample it later. Thank you.' He resumed his struggle with the champagne and finally the cork sprang from the neck of the bottle with a satisfying explosion and hit the tree, whereupon the lights went out yet again.

'Bull's-eye!' Bill exclaimed.

'Are you any good at getting them to stay on?'

'No way . . . I'm just the worst when it comes to gizmos like that,' he replied, betraying a Southern accent.

'Is this the first time you've both been in England?' Kate asked.

'Yes. Been here six months though.'

'Where're you both from?'

'Well, Harvey here is from the windy city, but I was born in Georgia, though my folks now live in Atlanta.'

'Oh, *Gone with the Wind*,' Kate said, then wished she hadn't.

'What d'you call the windy city?' Martin felt that he ought to get into the conversation.

'Chicago,' Harvey said.

'Just a Perrier for me,' Roger prompted.

'Having visited both, I much prefer Chicago to New York. I thought the museum was amazing,' Evelyn said.

'Yeah, I'm biased, but I agree, I think it's a great city.' Harvey lifted his glass. 'Well, Merry Christmas everybody, and thanks again for letting us share it with you.'

The conversation drifted into questions and answers about the differences between the two ways of life and comparisons of everyday goods and services.

'I was just flabbergasted at the price of gas,' Bill said. 'I mean, if they started charging us four dollars a gallon, why we'd just up and burn the White House.'

I can see why Jenny likes them, Kate thought. The old-fashioned word 'grace' came to mind, for within a very few minutes they had both eased themselves into a company of strangers without embarrassment, something the majority of Martin's friends could never do. Perhaps it stemmed from the American lack of class-consciousness, she thought; the fact that, without any snobbishness, they assumed they were as good as anybody else, whereas we British, with our outdated set of values and exaggerated respect for titles, are always on our guard. She was fascinated by Bill's Southern accent, his way of describing things as, now, he complimented her: 'I just love English houses, especially a home like this. I just think this is sharp as hens' teeth.' Harvey, the less extrovert of the two, volunteered to install Tony's new computer software and Tony took him off to his study.

'Are you brilliant at those things too, Bill? Tony gets into such a state when his machine deletes some pages of the book he's working on. I can't be doing with any of it,' Kate said. 'If it happened to me I'd take a hammer to the thing and that'd be the end of it.'

'I'm with you. It's a closed book I don't want to open.'

'There's nothing to them,' Martin chipped in. 'It's

just that Dad's machine is a museum piece. At least a year old.'

'There speaks the expert. So what're your interests, Bill?'

'Cooking.'

'Really? What sort of things d'you like cooking?'

' 'Most everything. I do a lot of Creole dishes and a mean bucatini pasta with pecorino cheese.'

'It's a fallacy that American food is uninteresting,' Evelyn said. 'I've always eaten great food over there. It's like everywhere else, you've got to know the right places. I had a perfectly disgusting meal in London last week, in a new place that was recommended in the *Telegraph*. Ghastly. Pretentious and an arm and a leg.'

'You should try Ziani's. That's where Harv and I go a lot.'

'Creole sounds way out of my league,' Kate said. 'I'm very much a throw-it-all-in-from-the door-and-hope-for-the-best sort of cook. As you'll find out shortly.'

'Don't you believe it,' Martin said, showing filial loyalty. 'Mum's a great cook. You should try my college food.'

'Sweet of you to stick up for me, darling, but it isn't true, I'm very average.'

'Can I take a peek at your kitchen?' Bill asked.

'Yes, if you want to. It's in a frightful mess.'

'Can I come?' Evelyn asked. 'D'you know Lee Bailey's cook-books?'

'Do I ever! Can you get him over here?'

'No, I don't think so. I bought mine in New York.'

'Lee's my Bible,' Bill said as they disappeared. 'I don't make a move without him. His chicken with Peach Salsa is not to be believed.'

'They've soon made themselves at home,' Martin said. Roger wrinkled his nose. 'But Americans are like that, aren't they? I haven't met that many, but those I have seem much more confident than us.' He wanted to sound knowledgeable.

'Too confident,' his uncle replied. 'Half the disasters in the world have come about because of their misguided belief that the almighty dollar can solve everything. Happily, events have proved them wrong.'

'The ones I've met have been very nice.'

'I like the way he went on about cooking considering that they've colonised the world with junk food.'

'McDonald's, you mean? I love a Big Mac. They make the best fries. You don't know what you're missing, uncle,' Martin said, the champagne, which he had drunk too quickly, slurring his words. 'Don't you like American films either?'

'I don't go to the cinema very often. Seldom anything worth seeing.'

'Didn't you even see *Basic Instinct*?'

'No.'

'That was terrific. I saw it three times.'

'What was so special about it?'

'Well, it was about this woman who killed her lovers, then the cop who was investigating the murders became involved with her, and there was a scene when they're questioning her – they suspect her but they've got no proof – and the woman, the girl, played by Sharon Stone, who was terrific, sat there in front of them and like, well, she wasn't wearing anything under her clothes, and you saw it all for a second.'

Roger stared at him. 'And that made it worth seeing, did it?'

'We all thought so.'

'Doesn't sound my cup of tea.'

Oh, sure, Martin thought, but I bet you go home and hire the video. He had long since decided that his uncle was a major nerd, and, emboldened by the champagne on a more or less empty stomach, he pressed home his enthusiasms. 'That and *The Silence of the Lambs* are my two favourites.'

'I'm amazed you have time to go to the cinema. I thought you were meant to be studying for a degree.'

'I am, but you've got to relax sometimes.'

'When you get out into the real world, Martin,' his uncle said, 'you'll realise that life is not anything like the cinema.'

'Who said it was? I know that. I do read the papers. That's why I'm enjoying myself while I can.' Even as he said it, a sliver of ice entered his mind, and he thought of the big question mark hanging over him. Oh, God, what if Patricia really was in the club? Ever since her phone call he had been trying to determine what his true feelings were. Evelyn had seemed the answer at the time, a new experience, but now memories of Patricia's pliant body flooded back. She might not have Evelyn's sophistication but she had other qualities, he didn't ever feel at a disadvantage with her. He suddenly gagged on the last of the champagne, the heated room swam, and he knew he was about to be sick.

'Excuse me,' he said, 'I just have to check on something.'

After he had thrown up he stayed kneeling on the bathroom floor, his head resting against the cold rim of the bowl, convinced that his life was over. If I get through this, he promised himself, I'll swear off sex and booze and really study. He pulled himself up and sluiced his mouth with cold water, raising his head to contemplate a stranger's face in the mirror. He felt engulfed by the unfathomable mystery of women and by remorse for his own culpability.

He was roused from further self-pity by a sudden commotion below. Going to the head of the stairs he saw his grandfather being helped inside by a strange man. Jenny and his mother were clucking around, and then his father and the others appeared, taking over from the stranger and supporting his grandfather into the living room. 'What's happened?' he shouted.

'Grandpa slipped on the ice as we came out of church,' Jenny said.

'Is he all right?'

'He's done his ankle in.'

Martin waited until his father had paid off the taxi-driver, then followed the others into the living room. His grandfather had been lowered into an armchair by the fire and Kate was removing his shoe and sock.

'Somebody ring Ted.'

'I'll do it,' Martin said.

'Silly of me,' Pop was saying. 'Always been very steady on my feet.'

'Could happen to anybody, Pop. Let me have a look. Put your foot up on this.' Exposed, his foot and ankle had already swollen to twice their normal size. 'Get some ice, Jenny, and have a look at the turkey while you're out there. Turn the oven down a notch just to be sure.'

Jenny kissed her friends on her way to the kitchen, saying, 'Hey! you two, great you made it, never a dull moment, eh? Catch up with you later.'

'These are the two boys from America Jenny told us about, Pop,' Kate explained.

'America, eh? That's the ticket. I'm usually up and about, not like this,' he said to them.

Harvey eased his obvious embarrassment. 'Could happen to anybody.'

'See if you can wiggle your toes,' Kate instructed. He did so and winced. 'Don't do it if it hurts.'

'D'you think it's broken?' Tony asked.

'No, I don't think so, more likely a bad sprain.'

'That's painful enough,' Bill said as Jenny returned with a bowl of ice cubes which they wrapped in a clean tea cloth and applied to the swelling.

'Be a bit cold going on, Pop, but bear with it.'

'I can stand pain, love. Pain never bothered me,' he said, but his face belied the boast.

'Ted's out on a call,' Martin reported. 'They're bleeping him.'

'You mean your doctor makes house calls?' Harvey exclaimed, as though such arcane practices could not possibly exist in today's world.

'Oh, yes.'

'You're kidding! Back home you could be dying of pneumonia and they'd still tell you to wrap up and come to emergency.'

'One hears nothing but horror stories about American medicine,' Roger said. 'I'm told that if you're unlucky enough to want a major operation you have to take out a second mortgage on your house.'

'Getting to be that way over here,' Tony said. 'We just happen to be fortunate that we've got an old-fashioned GP. How is it, Pop, the ice helping?'

'Yes, doing the trick, love. Dear, oh, dear, I was a silly boy losing my balance like that.'

'I bet you'll be up and about again in no time, Pop,' Jenny said. 'Tough old soldier like you.'

The word 'soldier' made Tony take a quick look at his wrist-watch, an action Kate wrongly thought to be a hint. 'Don't worry about lunch,' she said, 'nothing's spoiling.'

'Want me to take another look?' Bill volunteered.

'Would you?'

Tony beckoned his son. 'Come and help me bring in some logs.' When he had him alone he said: 'Never mind about the logs, go up into our bedroom and watch the news on our set. Then come and tell me.'

The doctor's Range Rover pulled up while Tony was still outside. 'Sorry to drag you out at lunchtime, Ted, but the old man took a nasty fall on the ice. I thought you ought to look at him.'

'Don't apologise. I need the business to pay for Christmas,' Ted said cheerfully, grabbing his bag from the front seat and following Tony into the house.

'Now then, Pop,' he said, 'what've you been up to? Been giving the communion wine a thrashing?'

'That's it,' the old man said, but they wondered whether he got the joke. Despite sitting close to the fire he had no colour in his face.

'Let's see what we've got here.' Ted removed the iced tea cloth; by now the ankle was disfigured with ugly purple blotches. Ted gently probed the swelling.

'Where does it catch you when I do that? Here . . . or here?'

'About there.'

'And what about when I do this?'

'That does it, yes.'

'Does what?'

'Gives it a bit of gyp.'

'How about the rest of you? Any pain in your back? What about your neck?' He felt with practised hands while talking.

'No.'

'Luckily, he landed in a snow-drift,' Jenny said.

Ted took Pop's blood-pressure and listened to his heart. Kate and Tony watched the doctor's face and he nodded at them before saying to his patient, 'Tell you what, Pop, let's go and take some pictures and make sure you haven't broken anything.' He packed his instruments away. 'I'll run him down to the cottage hospital. Has he got any slippers?'

'I'll get them,' Kate said.

'I'll go with Pop,' Jenny shouted after her. 'Don't suppose we'll be long.'

Collecting the slippers, Kate was on her way downstairs when she heard the television in their bedroom. 'What're you doing in here?' she asked her son.

'Dad told me to catch the news . . . they've blown up some soldiers.'

She stopped dead. 'Andy?'

95

'They didn't give names, not until next of kin have been informed.'

'Have you got his slippers?' Tony shouted from below.

'Yes, just coming.' She stared at the television; shots of the crater and the burnt-out armoured vehicle were on the screen. 'Don't for God's sake say anything to Jenny.'

'Course not.'

She dragged herself away.

'Have to call you Cinderella, Pop,' Jenny said, as they eased the slipper onto his foot. 'You shall go to the ball.'

Tony and Ted gave him a fireman's lift to the Range Rover.

'Sprains are a bitch,' Harvey remarked as they watched. 'Much more painful than a fracture. I know, I've had a few playing basketball. Don't look so worried, Mrs Chivers, I'm sure he'll be okay.'

'Yes, Ted's a good doctor, he doesn't take chances ... Pop pretends he can still get around as he used to, but we've noticed he's become very dodgy lately.' Her concern for him was genuine enough, but her thoughts were elsewhere ever since Martin had told her the news. 'Let's finish our champagne. Open another bottle, darling, we could all do with a refill after that ... I'll join you in a minute.' She left them and went into the kitchen. There she immediately picked up the phone and dialled 999. An operator responded. 'Police, Fire or Ambulance?'

'Police.'

'Can I have your name, please.'

'Chivers, Mrs Chivers.'

'And your number and where you're speaking from?'

Kate gave them.

'Stay on the line, please.'

There was a slight pause and then a woman police officer answered. 'Can you help me, officer?' Kate began. 'We've just seen the television . . . about the incident in Northern Ireland. And it's possible our son-in-law . . . he's an officer serving over there . . . it's possible he might be one of those involved. D'you have an emergency number I could ring?'

'Hold on, Mrs Chivers, I'll see.'

Tony came into the kitchen while she was waiting. He handed her a glass of champagne.

'Who're you ringing?'

'The police. I saw the news while I was upstairs. I'm trying to find out if there's a number we can call before Jenny gets back. Have they given any other details?'

'Four dead apparently and two others wounded.'

'Did they announce any names?'

He shook his head. 'D'you want something stronger than that?'

'I wouldn't mind.'

He poured some brandy from the bottle they were going to use on the Christmas pudding. She took a sip, coughed as it bit the back of her throat, then spoke into the phone. 'Yes? Oh, good.' Tony pushed a pencil and pad in front of her and she scribbled down the number. 'Thank you so much, I'm so sorry to have bothered you.' She looked down at the number and dialled again.

'It wouldn't necessarily be Andy's patrol. Probably one of many.'

'Then why hasn't he called her?'

She held the receiver close to her ear. 'Engaged.'

'I expect a lot of people are ringing.'

'I'll keep trying. You go back otherwise they'll think it odd.' She was dialling again as he left.

'I was just saying,' Harvey greeted him, 'there's nothing like a log fire, is there? Throws out a great heat.'

'Yes,' Tony agreed. 'Only trouble is it burns so quickly. We're lucky in one way, we lost half our trees in the big hurricane, so we've still got a ton of it.' He tried his best to be interested.

'Is it expensive over here? A cord of wood used to set my father back plenty.'

'Harvey and I discovered we've got a mutual friend,' Evelyn said. 'One of the faculty at the University of Chicago. I taught there for six months on an exchange programme.'

'It's a small world.'

'And shrinking,' Bill added. 'Have you caught these latest phones with a screen? You can see who you're talking to. Isn't that a horrible thought? Imagine, some old beau you dumped rings you and there's no escape.'

Tony noticed that his voice had moved up a pitch. 'No, I wouldn't care for that.' Except, he thought, it would solve everything if we could see Andy's face right now. Still distracted, he topped up their glasses, then said: 'Which reminds me, I must open the wine for lunch, let it breathe. Excuse me again.'

He went back to the kitchen. 'Did you get through?'

'Yes, but they wouldn't tell me anything.'

'Why not?'

'They'll only give out information to the named next of kin.'

'Why didn't you pretend you were Jenny?'

'I thought of it too late, by then I'd given them my own name. Why do they have to have such stupid rules?'

'I guess it's sensible. Could land them in trouble if they told the wrong people.'

'It's stupid,' she said and started to cry.

'Darling, don't let the others see you like that. Did you leave them this number?'

She nodded and wiped her eyes on a kitchen towel. 'What if it is him, what if Andy's dead, what will we do then?'

'Well, let's not assume the worst.'

'How can people do these things?'

Anguished himself and unable to answer the unanswerable, Tony paced a kitchen where every surface held utensils and food prepared for a celebration that now seemed irrelevant.

Six

As he killed time waiting for Jenny to return from the hospital, Tony thought back to all the other crises they'd lived through with the children: the meningitis scare with Martin when he was seven, Jenny falling out of the tree-house and lying unconscious for two hours, that and the long week agonising whether she might lose the sight in one eye when she was kicked by a pony. That had happened at Christmas, too, as if somebody decided the good things in life had to be evened-up on the scales. No matter how you tried, no matter how old your children were, you could never protect them from what life flung at them, there was always something new around the corner and your own experiences counted for little. New times threw up new hazards. He wasn't religious, there was no faith to cling to, but he found himself praying: let it be okay, don't deal that hand, please, give me some cards I can run with. But it was futile to speculate about divine intent; the die had been cast. He waited, half-hearing the small-talk around the fire, putting on an act for the strangers in their midst, but it was like listening to two crossed stations on the radio.

At the sound of the Range Rover returning he jumped up, knocking over his glass.

'Don't worry,' Bill said helpfully. 'It's champagne, it doesn't stain. I'll get a tissue and fix it.' But Tony hardly heard him. Opening the front door he saw Jenny coming up the path alone.

'They're keeping him in overnight for observation,' she said. 'Such a shame, poor old Pop, missing Mummy's lunch, but he seemed quite cheerful. I left him chatting up the nurses. You know what he's like when he's got a new audience.'

'Did they find anything?'

'Could be a hair-line fracture, and, as Ted said, at his age the thing they have to watch for is delayed shock.'

'Yes, that's right. Better be on the safe side.' He helped her off with her coat.

'Andy didn't ring while I was out, did he?'

'Not that I know of.'

'Well, you'd have heard. He is the end, never phones when he says he's going to. Where's Mummy?'

'In the kitchen.'

'I'll go and give her a hand. Is she in a state?'

'About what?' He could not keep the anxiety out of his voice, but Jenny appeared not to notice.

'Lunch. You know how she always gets and I guess you're all starving.'

As she entered the kitchen she was greeted with the sight of her mother kneeling in front of Bill wiping the front of his trousers.

'Oops! What happened?'

'I spilt turkey fat all down him. The bloody thing's so heavy, my wrist gave way as I was taking it out of the oven. Trying to do everything at once.'

'Just as well you explained. The position I found you both in could have been open to misinterpretation.'

'Well! Go wash your mouth out, young lady,' Bill said.

At any other time Kate would have seen the humour of the situation; now she just looked flushed and harassed. 'There! I think I got it all off, but they'll have to go to the cleaners.'

'No problem. Only a cheap pair of jeans.'

Kate straightened up and rushed to take the Brussels sprouts off the hob. 'God, everything's going wrong. How's Pop? Sorry, I should have asked right away.'

'They're keeping him in for a night, just to be sure.'

'Oh, dear, are they? Can you strain these, Bill? But nothing serious?'

'No, it's only a precaution. I'll do that, Mummy.

Don't get yourself in a tizz, everything's all under control. Just tell me what you want me to do.'

'Well, if you and Bill could get the bloody bird onto that dish and then stir the gravy, that would be a big help.'

'Nothing like making the guests work.'

'I love it,' Bill said, as between them they manoeuvred the turkey out of the pan. 'What a monster.'

'I was expecting three other people,' Kate said. 'And now Pop isn't going to be here either. I don't know, I can never gauge it properly.'

'Stop worrying,' Jenny said, 'just be more for the rest of us. It smells delicious.'

When, finally, they all sat down around the depleted table Kate could hardly swallow what she had cooked, although she made the effort for Jenny's sake. If Harvey and Bill were conscious of the tension they were well mannered enough to pretend otherwise, praising everything set before them, especially the flamed Christmas pudding, which both of them professed they had never eaten before.

'You've just gotta let me have the recipe,' Bill said. 'It's out of this world. And what's the sauce?'

'Rum butter.'

'No calories,' Jenny said.

'Oh, sure. A second on your lips, an inch on your hips.'

'Tell them how long ago you made this, Mummy.'

Kate looked up. 'Sorry?'

'The pudding. When did you make it?'

'Oh, that's one of last year's, I think.'

'How about that! Do you put them down like wine?'

'Sort of. They're better when they've stood.'

'How about that!' Bill repeated.

They pulled the crackers, put on the paper crowns that always split, read out the banal jokes, though watching her mother from time to time Jenny sensed something was odd.

'Are we going to watch the Queen's speech?' Roger asked.

Tony shot him a glance. 'I think we've missed it.'

'If Pop had been here we'd have been shot,' Jenny said. 'He takes it very seriously. When we were kids he made us stand up when they played the National Anthem, then we all had to drink a toast to the Queen. It was a big deal with him.'

'Wincarnis,' Tony said suddenly. 'It was always Wincarnis.'

'What's Wincarnis?' Harvey queried.

'A fortified wine. Pop swore by it. Slightly younger than what we're drinking now, I have to say.'

At that moment they heard the phone ring and Jenny jumped up. 'That'll be Andy, I'll get it.' She ran out of the room.

Tony looked across the table to Kate. Two white patches had appeared on her cheeks, a warning sign he knew well. She suddenly pushed back her chair.

'It's no good,' she said, 'I've got to go and find out what's happening.' She went after Jenny.

'Is something wrong?' Harvey asked in the silence.

Tony hesitated, then said, 'Yes. Something's come up which might mean bad news. I hope not, but at the moment we don't know. I may as well tell you, because one way or another you're going to find out. The IRA exploded a bomb this morning which killed four British soldiers.'

'Oh, Jesus! And you think one of them might be Andy?'

'Well, it's strange he didn't call as promised. We saw it on the news earlier, but we've been keeping it from Jenny in the hope that he'd ring her and say he was okay. Look, if you'll excuse me, I'd better go, too, just in case. Don't you come, Martin, stay here.'

After he left the room the remaining four sat very still, as though the slightest movement could somehow affect the outcome.

Tony found Jenny and Kate in the living room by the phone. Kate had her arms around her daughter. They were both crying, though whether from grief or relief he had no immediate means of telling. His voice came out with a croak as he forced himself to ask the question: 'What did they say?' Kate shook a hand at him over Jenny's shoulder. 'Well, I must know,' he said.

'It *was* Andy's patrol,' Kate said. 'But he's not dead, just badly concussed. Apparently he wasn't in the vehicle when the thing went off . . . He left his men there while he went ahead on his own to investigate something suspicious.'

'Thank God!' He went to them and bundled them all together in his arms, feeling his daughter's tears mingling with his own.

'Oh, Daddy, d'you think he'll be all right?'

'I'm sure, baby.'

'Concussion isn't fatal, is it?'

'No, course not.'

'I mean, they get over it, don't they?'

'Promise you.'

'They helicoptered Andy and the other boy.'

'Listen, he'll be getting the best treatment. They have great doctors with plenty of experience treating those kind of injuries.'

'I'm going over there,' Jenny said.

'Of course you must,' he agreed.

'Can you get me on a plane? Any plane, I don't care.'

'Leave it to me.'

'I don't have enough money with me.'

'Don't worry about that, I'll take care of it . . . You want me to go with you?'

She shook her head. 'No, I'd rather go on my own.'

'You sure now, wouldn't you feel better if I was with you?'

'No, I'll be fine, I just want to get there.'

'Okay, well you go and put what things you need

together, while I call the airport. Kate, just go in and explain to the others what's happening.' He was galvanised and clear-headed now that they knew what they were dealing with. 'You're absolutely sure you wouldn't rather I came too?'

'No, Daddy, don't make me cry again. Thanks, but no.' She said it vehemently as though whatever she found at the end of her journey, she had to face it alone. He knew that feeling, it was part of his own make-up, the need to take one's blurred, burnt-out emotions away from everybody. Perhaps that was why a lot of people committed suicide in anonymous hotel rooms in cities far from home.

Seven

Browning slush hissed under the Volvo's tyres as Tony drove back from Heathrow. There was little traffic on the motorway – the weather and the annual 'Don't Drink and Drive' campaign seemed to have kept most people by their firesides. Heathrow, too, had been uncharacteristically deserted, just a few air-crews who had drawn the short straw on their rota and small knots of West Indians and Pakistanis, bundled with their possessions. He had no problem getting Jenny on the Belfast flight for there were few takers for that city on Christmas Day. Although Tony had never been there, two decades of newsreel footage had made its streets familiar to him; kissing his daughter goodbye at the barrier he carried away a vivid picture of where she would sleep that night, if sleep she did. She was calm when they parted, calmer than he, as if their roles had been reversed and now it was he who needed comfort. It was only on the journey home that he felt able to let go; tears distorted his vision and he made curious choking noises, amplified in the closed car, crying as he had not done since a child. He pulled over into a lay-by until he recovered, then lit a cigarette, wanting to delay as long as possible the return to a house that had been half-emptied.

During the last part of the journey his thoughts moved to Martin and he began silently to rehearse what he needed to say and do there. It seemed that in the space of twenty-four hours their entire lives had been turned inside out, that the luck they usually enjoyed in comparison to most had deserted them.

After the minor success of his first novel, Tony had managed to keep the creative adrenalin flowing, producing a new book every year, never hitting the big time, but, with the paperback and some foreign editions, making enough to keep them comfortable – enough for a decent car and an annual holiday, usually in the South of France, where, in his heart, he hankered to retire. The England he had once thought held all that he cherished had become, during the Thatcher years, a country of hideous contrasts. When they had first moved to the Chalfonts, leaving their cramped city flat for a first taste of the good life (aping a popular television sit-com of the period), they had never given a thought to security; for the first seven years they had seldom locked the doors at night. Now the inner city violence had spread into the countryside; their insurance premiums (not that they had anything worth stealing) had trebled, an alarm system was now mandatory and a constant source of worry. 'If the cat farts,' Kate was fond of saying, 'the bloody thing goes off and we have to play midnight host to the police.' Parking meters and the rightly resented clamp had appeared in the local shopping parade where, recently, the owner of the wine store had been knifed in broad daylight and the men's outfitters ram-raided. Every week the local rag carried stories of masked intruders assaulting and raping elderly citizens, alongside statistics showing meagre conviction rates of the perpetrators. More and more, Tony felt a sense of unease when they retired to bed, kept the car doors locked when driving and hoarded an illegal canister of Mace, smuggled in by a friend. He felt saddened that all the old bastions had been stormed by scandal – the Royal family, the City, the national sports – as though a tapeworm of corruption had lodged itself in the bowels of a society once revered for its ability to withstand all ills. An increasingly nihilistic tabloid Press pandered to a common denominator that was off the scale, revelling in the undistinguished, the tawdry, anything that could hasten the slide. It was as though somebody had decided to pull the plug on tradition, on all those carefully honed, civilised attributes that other countries had tried to emulate, and substitute in their place a society where the second-rate was king.

It began to snow again and Tony boosted the heater, slowing down as he left the motorway and hit the deserted and more treacherous rural streets. There was a hypnotic quality to the snowflakes as they arrived and melted on the windscreen. He pondered on the events of the day. Santa Claus had certainly brought a sackful of goodies this holiday – a son-in-law and father in hospital, a brother responding to the call of Mohammed and a son with a pregnant girlfriend. Looking at the lighted windows he passed, he wondered if such glad tidings of comfort and joy had been bestowed on others. Why me, he thought, why have I been singled out? His concentration momentarily lapsed as he turned the last corner and he felt the car lose traction and start to slide at an angle across the road. Panic elongated the seconds into hours before he finally corrected the skid. He was in a cold sweat by the time he had successfully parked the car in the garage. Kate found him still sitting there smoking a cigarette.

'What're you doing?' she said.

'I was considering whether to attach a hosepipe to the exhaust. What does it look like I'm doing?'

'Don't snap at me, darling. I was worried about you. Did she get off all right?'

'Yes.'

'How was she?'

'Okay, I think. In better shape than me. I guess it's always better when you've made a decision. It's the waiting that gets you. She promised to ring and let us know how he is the moment she gets there. Anything more on the news?'

'I didn't put it on. Come in. You can't sit there, the others will wonder what the hell's wrong.'

He extinguished his cigarette and got out of the car. 'What else has happened here?' he asked as they went inside, an irrational resentment against a return to domesticity welling up inside him. 'Has Roger been giving readings from the Koran to keep your spirits up?'

'No, I must say, he's behaved very well. Still no booze, and actually joined in the conversation at one point.'

'Ah, well.'

'Do you think he's having second thoughts about it all? Have you talked any more to him?'

'Haven't had a chance. I thought about his situation when I was sitting out there contemplating my navel. How's Pop, by the way, did you ring?'

'He's okay, running a bit of a temperature, but the sister said they're watching him. I talked to Pop as well and he seems to be having a high old time. Lots of pretty nurses and it's all wonderful, so that's a relief because I felt so sorry about him missing everything.'

'Come here.' He hugged her. 'I'm sorry.'

'I hate it when you're all snappy,' she said.

'I wasn't getting at you, but it's been such a long, lousy day and I had a skid which shook me up.'

'Well, you didn't have to take it out on me. It hasn't exactly been *Noel's House Party* here since you left.'

'I'd love some coffee.'

'Well, that's fresh. I just made it for the others.'

Tony poured himself a cup. 'Our two visitors from the colonies must be wondering what they walked into. Come and enjoy an English Christmas, I don't think.'

'They've been very sweet. Bill helped with the washing-up.' She lowered her voice. 'You don't think he's gay, do you?'

'That's the criterion, washing-up?'

'No. Just one or two things he let slip. I don't think they're a twosome, though I suppose they could be. I must ask Jenny when I next see her. Hasn't this been the weirdest Christmas? What else could happen?'

'Well, if you're right, Bill could make a pass at me. That might round it off. Or Evelyn maybe. She's more my type.'

'Is she?'

'No, course not, idiot.'

'I actually quite like her. I didn't at first, but she grows on you, though I still think she's too old for Martin. We ought to go and join them.'

'Yes.' He stared at the half-eaten turkey on the kitchen island. 'You ever thought, the whole country's going to be on a cold turkey jag for the next month?' He put on a voice. 'Would you like scrambled eggs for breakfast, dear? No thanks, I'll have turkey. What about lunch? Oh, turkey I think, don't you? And dinner? Darling do we have any of that cold turkey left? . . . They have a sad life, don't they? Born ugly, get fattened up, and then, curtains. Nobody ever writes nice things about them. I mean, Beatrix Potter never featured them like Peter Rabbit, did she? They just become anonymous corpses.'

'Well, there's your chance. Write a children's book about them next.'

'*The Tale of Timothy Turkey . . . The Adventures of Gus the Gobbler . . .* ' he mused. 'No, that sounds vaguely pornographic.'

'Perhaps that's what every publisher is waiting for. Oh, I'm glad I've got you. If I was married to some-body like Roger I wouldn't wait for him to take off, his bags would be in the street.'

The fug in the living room, a mixture of cigarettes and a wood fire that had been burning since morning, immediately enveloped him. Not for the first time Tony thought what a nice room it was to come home to, not 'sharp as hens' teeth' as Bill described it, a little dated maybe, the covers on the armchairs shabby, the paintwork in need of a fresh coat, but the general effect, enhanced by all of Kate's Christmas decorations, comfortable. And that's what he wanted to be again. Comfortable. The day's events started to recede as soon as he sat down.

'Boy! does that fire feel good,' he said, as Kate put a whisky in his hand.

'Was she okay?' Evelyn was the first to enquire. 'We've been so worried.'

'Fine. She was fine. I was the one in a state. Like seeing her off to school for the first time.'

'You've got to hand it to Jenny,' Bill said, 'going alone like that. That was really spunky.'

'She did the right thing,' Evelyn said. ' I remember when my ex got ill abroad – he had to travel on business a lot – and he was in the Gambia in some God-awful spot when he caught one of those frightful bugs, and of course he'd have died if I hadn't gone and got him out. Like Jenny, I just got on the first plane and went.'

It was the first time a husband had been mentioned and both Kate and Tony registered it somewhat obviously.

'I've heard that Gambia is the worst,' Tony said as conversationally as he could.

'Yes, I read an article in one of my magazines the other week which you wouldn't believe,' Kate said.

'What was that, Kate?' Harvey asked.

'Well, apparently planeloads of British women, no longer in the full flush of youth, shall we say? go out there to get bonked.'

'Really?'

'Really. I showed it to you, didn't I, Tony? Because he thought I was making it up.'

'True,' Tony agreed. 'There was a full-page photo spread showing some prime examples of advanced cellulite doing a bit of leg-over on the beaches with local toy boys. One caption quoted a grandmother from Hull saying her date had shown her a piece of Africa. "Piece" being the operative word. I cancelled Katy's passport as a precaution.'

'I went to Tangier once,' Bill chipped in, 'after I saw that film and got a yen for some of that old desert moon stuff.'

'Which film was that?'

'*The Sheltering Sky*, with Winger and Malkovich. It bombed, I gather, but I loved it.'

'Oh, yes,' Tony said, 'from the Bowles novel. We missed it somehow, didn't we, darling? I must get the video.'

'*The Dream at the End of the World*,' Evelyn commented.

'Sorry?'

'It's the title of a recent biography of Bowles and his set.'

'So what about Tangier, Bill?' Kate asked, making an effort to steer the conversation away from what she was really thinking. 'Did it live up to your expectations?'

There was a certain hesitancy before Bill answered. 'Well, what I expect out of life and what I get are usually two different things. Let's just say it didn't prove to be my "dream at the end of the world".'

'The romance of travel ain't what it used to be,' Tony said. 'Kate and I were once seduced by one of those brochures they pop through the letter box and signed up for a winter cruise.'

'Tell us,' Harvey said, 'I've often been tempted. They all look so glamorous.'

'Well, on ours the crew were straight out of the cast of *Treasure Island* and we got Blind Pew as our cabin steward.'

'And tell them about the rest of the passengers,' Kate prompted.

'I suppose we'd fondly imagined it'd be Mardi Gras every night, gourmet food, top entertainment and lots of bright young things living it up.' Tony paused for effect. 'No way. It was God's floating waiting room, crammed with geriatrics, most of whom had come on board to die. I'm not exaggerating. We had to sit at the same table for every meal with two couples who should have been on life-support machines. It's true that a few of them were fit enough to play deck quoits, but there was always the danger that it could be their last throw.'

'Didn't you go ashore at all?'

'Yeah, and that was a mixed blessing too. On one occasion they anchored off an island on the coast of Africa entirely populated with ex-Nazis. Try and imagine a naked Nuremberg Rally staged on a beach and you'll get the picture.'

'What about the entertainment, I thought those

118

cruises always had great shows on board?' Harvey asked.

'Not this one. We had a female ventriloquist with a Maggie Thatcher doll – very topical, then a comedian dressed in a kilt who told Jewish jokes in an Irish accent. The highlight was the fancy-dress parade. And, by the way, the first prize was another cruise, so we didn't exactly scramble to enter. They had to make their own costumes and the theme was "Film Stars". So of course we had half a dozen Charlie Chaplins, one of whom fell off the stage and broke his leg, at least three transvestite Scarlet O'Haras . . . '

'Stop!' Bill screamed. 'Who won?'

'Some old guy who wrapped himself in a toilet roll and came on as the Invisible Man.'

'And you say you didn't have a laugh?'

'By then we were too exhausted to laugh. We had to take another holiday to get over it, didn't we, darling?'

Kate nodded. 'Jenny must be there by now,' she said, her thoughts still with her daughter. As if answering her prayers, at that very moment the phone rang and she rushed to answer it.

'Darling, you got there all right? . . . How is he? . . . Oh, thank God for that. Let me tell the others . . . ' She turned back into the room. 'They don't think Andy has any permanent injury. That's the news we've been waiting for, darling. Was he conscious? . . . Oh, good, so he knows you're there. Be sure and give him

119

our love . . . Where are you now? . . . I see, and you say they're going to let you stay in the hospital tonight? . . . D'you want to give us that number?' She gestured for a pencil which Harvey supplied and she scribbled the number down. 'Well, ring us again in the morning and reverse the charges. Darling, I'm so relieved for you. If there's anything you want, let us know. All my love. Take care of yourself too.'

She was between joy and tears when she put the phone down. 'Sorry, I can't help it, and I haven't got a handkerchief.'

'Here,' Tony said. 'And he's definitely okay?'

'Yes, very shaken up and bruised, but he's had a brain scan and there's no serious damage.'

'That's great. The other good thing is they're bound to ship him home when he leaves hospital.'

'Marvellous news,' Roger said.

'I'm glad we were still here,' Harvey said. 'I'd have been awake all night, but I think now we really ought to be going, don't you think, Bill?'

'Yeah, you're right.'

They both got up. 'Wouldn't you like some more coffee and something to eat before you go?' Kate said.

'You must be kidding. I'm gonna go on a diet for a week.'

'Well, let me put some coffee in a Thermos for the journey.'

'Honestly, no. We'll be fine.'

But when Tony saw them to the front door the snow

120

drifts were two feet high and it was still coming down heavily. 'You can't drive in that,' he said. 'Stay the night.'

'Well . . . '

'Honestly, I wouldn't go out in that unless I had to, and you don't know our roads.'

'Won't that be very inconvenient, though?'

'No, no problem.' As they came back inside and closed the door he shouted to Kate: 'Darling, it's a blizzard out there, so the boys are going to stay the night.'

'Is that okay, Kate?' Bill asked.

'Course it is.' She made it sound genuine. 'I'll go put some clean sheets on.'

'Let me help,' Evelyn said. They both went upstairs.

'I feel terrible,' Harvey said. 'We were only invited for lunch.'

'It's Christmas. Come back in the warm and I'll open a bottle to celebrate.'

Roger joined Tony in the kitchen. 'Corkscrew?' Tony said. 'Where's the corkscrew? Look in that drawer.'

As Roger handed it to him he said: 'I've made a mess of things, haven't I?'

'It'll all work out. Give it time.'

'Have you and Kate ever had a serious row?'

'God, yes.'

'I mean, really serious. The sort that makes you want to end it all?'

'Yes, when we're really angry. I'm a nightmare to live with sometimes. Shit! half the bloody cork's gone in the bottle.'

Roger said, 'Let me. I'm good at that.' He took the bottle from his brother. 'It's all a question of pride, isn't it? You and I always get off on the wrong foot, don't we? I wish I knew why.'

'Probably because we don't see each other often enough. Must be ages since we had a night on the town alone together.' Looking at his brother Tony's thoughts went back to the days when they had shared a room – their beds set L-shaped, head to head, in the house where they had both been brought up. He remembered their nightly squabbles, the rivalry, the differences that had shaped their early lives.

'I get the feeling that you despise me,' Roger said.

'That's not true. God, how awful if you think that.'

'It's just that we've never understood each other. When I read your books I never know what to say about them, it's like discovering somebody I never knew. Some of the things you write shock me.'

'Shock you?'

'Yes. I don't mean in the conventional sense. They shock me because they describe emotions I've never experienced. You can write about love, and I don't think I've ever known love. I envy what you and Kate have.'

'I just got lucky. Whether Kate's so lucky is another matter. It's no fun being married to a writer.'

'Don't you ever want to live your life over?'

'Of course, who doesn't?'

'So what's the answer?'

'What's the question, as Gertrude Stein said. Hell, I don't know, all I do know is we all have to play the hand we're dealt. You either bluff or fold. I guess I bluff my way through most things.'

'Yes,' Roger said. 'But sometimes that's not enough, is it?'

They both had no idea how to end the conversation; the sleeping emotions they had released embarrassed them.

'Well, let's have that stag lunch,' Tony said as they went to rejoin Harvey and Bill. 'Make it our New Year's resolution. On me.'

Eight

'You and Tony don't approve of me, do you?' Evelyn said.

The question took Kate off-guard, but even as she searched for a polite way to respond she admitted the truth of it to herself: it wasn't so much approval or disapproval, more a resentment towards this woman who was somehow closer to her son than she was.

'As far as Tony and I are concerned Martin's old enough to choose his own friends,' she said.

'But preferably from his own age group, isn't that what you'd really like to say?'

Kate stopped stripping the bottom sheet off one of the twin beds. This is the last thing I need right now, she thought, I can do without this. She made an effort to take the abrasiveness out of her voice when next she spoke. 'With both Jenny and Martin we've tried to remember something I read once, something Enid

Bagnold wrote in her autobiography . . . She said how important it was for children to have secrets from their parents. Not always easy to accept, but it saves a lot of upset.'

Evelyn picked up the discarded sheet and folded it, both women occupying themselves with the mundane task while thinking of something else. 'I didn't want you to think I wasn't aware that it was fairly crass of me to turn up uninvited, but until we were half-way here I'd no idea Martin hadn't warned you in advance.'

'Well, don't feel badly about that. That's typically Martin. He always treats this place like a hotel.' Now leave it, Kate said to herself, don't go on, it's been a long day, first with Pop and then with Jenny's news.

But Evelyn wanted it all out in the open. 'If I can just explain, being around younger people all the time, the lines get blurred. Not that I was on the prowl for a toy boy, don't think that, far from it, I was just very flattered that somebody like Martin found me interesting. But I should have had more sense, after all what is age for if not to have a bit of savvy?'

Kate plumped a pillow. 'Okay, if we're going to be frank with each other, can I ask you something? Is this an ongoing thing?'

'I don't know. Would it upset you if we were?'

'Yes,' Kate said, 'I guess it would, to be honest.

That probably makes me very old-fashioned, doesn't it?'

'Not really. He's your son, I'm sure a divorced older woman is not what you had in mind for him . . . Well, to set your mind at rest, and I know what you've been through today, it's just a friendship, maybe open to misinterpretation, but that's all it is. I hope you can believe me.'

'Yes, of course I do, I'm sorry. Like you said, it's not been the greatest day, and I'm tired. I didn't mean to sound aggressive. Mothers are supposed to be closer to boys, aren't they? But Martin grew away from me as soon as he went to boarding-school. Perhaps that was the mistake we made. Now I've no idea what goes on inside his head. Are they all like that?'

'I don't know, I haven't got much to go on.'

'You never had children of your own?'

'No, not my own. We adopted a little girl once, but there's a probationary period, as I'm sure you know, before the papers become final – the real mother can change her mind and apply to have the child back.'

Kate stopped what she was doing. 'Is that what happened in your case?'

'Yes. I won't pretend that was the reason my marriage broke up, but I suppose it contributed – well, I know it did.'

They looked at each other across the partially made

bed. 'I can't imagine something like that,' Kate said. 'That would kill me.'

'Well, I don't think about it much any more. Just occasionally I wonder where she is and what she's like now. Anyway, that's enough of me. The important thing is Jenny's good news.'

'When he didn't ring I really thought he was dead,' Kate said, wishing she could say something that would make up for her previous lack of charity. She surveyed the bed. 'There. I must get them some clean towels. I suppose they won't mind sleeping in the same room? Tony and I wondered if they're a twosome. What d'you think?'

'It did enter my mind when Bill talked about Tangier. It's always been a gay hunting ground.'

'Well, nothing we can do about it. There's no more room at this inn. Thanks, that was a big help. I hope you're okay in that little room. Were you comfortable last night? There're extra blankets if you weren't.'

'I slept like a log.'

'Why do we say that – "slept like a log"? D'you think it started out as "slept like a hog"?'

'It never occurred to me, but you're probably right.'

Kate smoothed the newly made bed. 'Funny how one thinks more about it these days. I never used to.'

'What's that?'

'Well, gays, Aids. Tony and I talk about it a lot. Because of Martin, I suppose. I feel sorry for anybody his age.' The words were out before she could stop herself. 'Well age doesn't come into it, of course,' she added. 'It affects everybody, even babies are born with it now. Such a savage God, if there is a God, to dump that on us just for making love . . . Come on, we've had enough gloom for one day, let's you and me go and have a drink on our own.'

She picked up the soiled bed-linen, took a last look around, then, the room tidied to her satisfaction, they went downstairs.

'I had a long talk with Evelyn this evening,' Kate said when they were in bed, 'and I think I misjudged her.'

Tony was reading a book. 'Good,' he murmured.

'Turns out she's had a sad life. And where Martin's concerned we got it all wrong. They're just good friends.'

'Good.'

'She said they're not sleeping together, and I believed her.'

Another 'Good,' barely audible.

'Are you listening?'

'Yes, you said they were good friends.' He turned a page. 'Course, I doubt that's all there is to it.'

'What d'you mean?'

'Just that.'

'Why not?'

'Not possible. No normal man, and certainly nobody Martin's age, can just be "good friends" with any woman.'

'What a fatuous generalisation.'

'I'm telling you. When the sap is rising, as I imagine it is with Martin, any relationship has a basis of sex.'

'Balls!'

'Okay, have it your way. You're right and I'm wrong.' He went back to his book. Kate was silent for a few moments, then she said: 'I can't believe you said that.'

'Forget it, it's not important.'

'But I want to know *why* you said it. You must have had a reason.'

He put his book down with a sigh. 'Well, it's obvious he's attracted to her otherwise she wouldn't be here.'

'I suppose it wouldn't occur to you he could be attracted to her mind? She's extremely intelligent and well read.'

'So was Madame de Staël.'

'What's she got to do with it?'

'She drove Benjamin Constant crazy. Older woman, younger man. Why are we discussing this?'

'Because of what you said. You said . . . '

'I know what I said. It just happens to be my opinion. You disagree. End of argument. Now can I finish this?'

'You're so pedantic sometimes.' There was another silence. 'She told me that one of the professors took her out a couple of times and then asked her to wear a black rubber suit.'

'And did she?'

'No, of course she didn't.' Kate turned over in bed and stared at him until he reluctantly took notice.

'Now what?'

'What will you say to him?'

'Who?'

'Martin, of course. You've got to sort the situation out.'

'I intend to.'

'What will you say?'

'I haven't decided yet.' He was still reading.

'If she is pregnant something has to be done in a hurry. She's the one we've got to consider.'

Tony put his book down. 'Darling, haven't we had enough dramas for one day? Let's not go into it now, please. You're tired, we're both tired, don't let's fight.'

'I'm not fighting. I'm just concerned that's all, and I just want to get our lives straight.'

'We will.'

'You say that, but you don't do anything.'

'What d'you want me to do, wake him up, roust him out of bed? Be reasonable. I will talk to him tomorrow, I promise, but get it into proportion. He might ... I say "might" ... have got a girl in the family way. That's a problem if it's true, but it's solvable. We're lucky we've had some good news today, we could be lying here with Andy dead and Jenny crying her eyes out.'

'What d'you mean "solvable"?'

'Well, there are three possibilities – options, if you like. "A" it's a false alarm, and we can all relax, "B" they get married and have the baby or "C".'

'What's "C"? You mean abortion?'

'Yes.'

'Easy enough to say if you're a man.'

'Darling, I'm not advocating abortion, just stating facts.'

'But the way you said it means you do think it's easy.'

'No. As a matter of fact I don't. If you must know I question whether any man has the right to enter the argument.'

After another pause Kate said: 'He obviously wasn't practising safe sex.'

'Well, obviously not safe enough.'

'I blame Martin.'

'Yes and no. It takes two . . . '

'Don't give me that old thing. It isn't a tango, it's a baby.' Kate lapsed into silence again, but the fact that he resumed reading annoyed her. 'If you think about it, it's all unjust. There's Evelyn who desperately wanted a baby, but couldn't have one, and that irresponsible son of ours fertilising everything in sight.'

'Slight exaggeration.'

'What d'you think will happen?'

'I don't know, do I?' Tony said patiently, well aware that the conversation could drift into an all night session. 'All I can say is I'll do my best to work it out for them.'

'Do you think her parents know?'

'Doubtful, from what Martin said.'

'What else did he tell you then? Why do I have to prise it out of you one word at a time? Why are you so secretive?'

'I'm not. You know as much as I do.' Turning another page, he added: 'The only other thing he told me is that her parents are Catholic.'

'There you are! Why not come out and say that?'

'I've just said it. Jesus God Almighty, what's got into you?'

'Well, that's it! She'll have to have it, Martin'll have to marry her.'

'Fine. End of story.'

'How can you be so complacent? You just accept it, do you? Just like that?'

'Kate, darling, you're the one who just said he'll have to marry her. You said that, not me. Now, maybe he will, maybe he won't, I don't have the gift of second sight like you.'

'Why d'you have to turn so narky?'

'Because this is a ridiculous argument.' He turned out his bedside light. 'Last night your big concern was whether he and Evelyn were having it off – she was the problem – now it appears you wish they were.'

'I didn't say that.'

'You implied it.'

'Well, at least Evelyn would be mature enough to deal with it. She's a very sensible woman.'

'Even sensible women get pregnant. You're a case in point. Jenny wasn't exactly planned.'

'That's different. We were married.'

'Darling, you carried more than a bouquet up the aisle.'

'Thanks. Thanks a lot. You really know how to twist the knife.' She sat up, bunched her pillow savagely and lay down again. 'Sweetheart, I wasn't getting at you,' Tony said, placatingly. 'Don't let's have a row, it's always a mistake to get into these things late at night. I haven't got a magic wand I can wave, I wish I had. I'm as concerned as you are, and I'll do my best to find the right answer.'

'Okay,' she said quietly.

'I'm sorry I made that crack.'

'That's okay.'

'Forgive me?'

'Yes.'

'It's life I guess. We just seem to have had a basinful lately . . . Kids . . . I'm the same as you, I lie here sometimes, wondering when the next blow will fall . . . Is the bloody novel any good? How long can we afford to stay here? Should I do anything about the boiler before it blows up in our faces? . . . It isn't that I deliberately don't tell you everything . . . no point in pushing all my boring worries onto you, that doesn't make them come right, does it?'

He raised his head slightly to look at her. The regularity of her breathing told him she was asleep.

Nine

'We've run out of milk,' Kate said as Tony made a groggy entrance into the kitchen the following morning.

'Have we?' He swayed and stubbed his toe. 'Right, when I go to the hospital later, I'll see if the garage has any. That'll be the only place likely to be open. As we know the powerhouse of industry known as England shuts down until the New Year . . . Did I drink too much last night?'

'Probably.'

'Where's the coffee?'

'Where it always is.'

He looked. 'But the pot's empty.'

'So make some fresh. Turn around, face the fridge, open it, and see if a tin marked "Coffee" stares back at you.'

'Why're you being sarcastic?'

'Because every day you say, "Where's the coffee?"'

as if I hide it in a fresh place deliberately to confuse you.'

He mooched around for the next five minutes, a misjudged man moving in slow motion. 'Are the others up?'

'Evelyn is. She's very kindly vacuuming the living room. Saves you offering,' she added in the same tone of voice she had used earlier.

'I would have done it if you'd asked me.'

'Some people do it without being asked.'

He measured the ground coffee into a jug with an unsteady hand. 'Have you fed the cat?'

'Yes, I gave her the turkey scraps.'

'Should have given her the whole lot.' He poured the hot water in and stirred.

'You haven't forgotten what you're going to do this morning?'

'No, I have it in the front of my mind. That and a headache.'

'The sooner you do it the better.'

'Milk?' he muttered when he had poured the coffee, lost again.

'I just told you, we haven't got any. What we did have was left out and went off.'

'Are you in a bad mood?'

'No.'

'Seem to be. Have I upset you? Something I said?'

'No, as a matter of fact you were very funny when

you came back last night. You can be funny when you want to.'

'Meaning I'm not now?'

She stopped what she was doing and faced him. 'Tony, take your coffee, go into your study and let me get on. I've got a lot to do and I can't do it with you under my feet.'

Before leaving he felt the top of the boiler to test whether it was still working. The sound of the Hoover as he made his way to his sanctuary was as painful to his ears as the music of Stockhausen. He sat behind his desk and looked at the neat pile of manuscript. The thought of having to resume work held no enchantment, but he turned to the last page, read where he had left off, then, out of long habit, took a pencil, crossed out a few lines of dialogue and made a note in the margin. Like most writers he needed to give himself a trigger in order to start again. Was this the one that was going to make their fortune? He doubted it. The stale aftermath of Christmas loomed ahead, that dreary end to the year when everything took on the appearance of a remnant sale and the creative juices flowed slowly. He lit a cigarette, immediately regretted it, but persevered – real addicts did not surrender easily. At any moment now, he thought, the bills will start flooding in. No matter what urgent personal mail got delayed in the Christmas post, credit card accounts, tax demands and the like were linked to their own Wells Fargo: they always got through.

As he surveyed the room, what lay ahead of him seemed as devoid of cheer as the ashes in the grate. The blank screen of his word processor reflected a face that had never pleased him: too round, lacking the creases he felt his burdens should have implanted, lines which bestowed a certain weather-beaten dignity commensurate with a literary reputation. Not Auden, that was going too far, but Graham Greene perhaps, so that his photograph on dust-jackets would make reviewers think twice before slamming him. The coffee was filthy and he left it undrunk, getting up from his desk to take a closer look at himself in a mirror. I shall be Peter Pan all my life, he thought. The events of yesterday should have aged me overnight, but apart from the stubble I'm still revoltingly cherubic. He wondered whether he should grow a beard, take the Hemingway route, except that, knowing his luck, the bloody thing would only grow in sparse patches, like a field where the fertiliser had missed in places. In addition he had always felt that beards gave an artsy-fartsy appearance, the sort that earnest directors at the Royal Court sported, but all the same there was something to be said for covering up the blandness of his features.

As he sat there he heard the front door slam. Swivelling in his chair he was surprised to see Roger get into his car and drive off. Tony went back to the kitchen.

'Roger's gone.'

'I know.'

'Without saying anything? Bloody rude.'

'He said good morning to me.'

'I wanted to see him before he went.'

'Well, he's coming back.'

'Coming back?'

'Yes, he told me he was just going to a meeting.'

'Going to a meeting?'

'Yes, Tony, don't repeat everything I say. A meeting, that's what he said.'

'Nobody has a meeting on Boxing Day.'

Tony wandered back to his study and was drinking the remainder of his cold, black coffee and pondering Roger's latest eccentricity when Martin poked his head around the door. 'There's no milk, Dad,' he said.

'So I have discovered.'

'I won't be able to have cornflakes.'

'Have turkey instead.'

'Turkey? Why would I have turkey for breakfast?'

'Some people would be very grateful for turkey at any meal.'

Searching for an ashtray Tony finally doused his cigarette in his coffee cup and got up. 'As soon as I've found my face and shaved, I'm going to the hospital. Come with me in case the car gets stuck. We'll get some milk on the way home.'

'Oh. Evelyn and I were going for a walk.'

'You can go for a walk this afternoon. I need to talk to you. And you need to talk to me. We both need to talk to each other, wouldn't you say? I'll be ready in twenty minutes.'

The driveway had to be cleared of banked snow before Tony could get the Volvo out on the road. 'Put your belt on,' he said, 'in case we skid.' The sky was still heavy with more snow to come, and Tony needed skill to keep the car in a straight line. Despite his overnight rehearsals, he was still searching for the right words with which to open the dialogue about Patricia's situation.

'Have you had any further thoughts?' he began.

'What about?'

'What d'you think? Patricia, of course.'

'Not really.'

'Does Evelyn know?'

'Sort of.'

'Well, does she or doesn't she?'

'I did mention it, yes.'

'And?'

'You've got the wrong idea about Evelyn. I just like her as a friend. I'm not involved or anything like that.'

'So I gathered from your mother. She and Evelyn had a talk last night.'

Martin clutched the dashboard as they turned a corner. 'About me?'

'Who else?'

The back wheels spun at that moment, temporarily putting a stop to the subject. It wasn't until Tony had regained control and they both breathed again that Martin said: 'I don't know why people have to talk about me behind my back.'

'As you get older, Martin, you'll realise that the only conversations worth having are behind people's backs. That revelation may come to you slowly, but it will come, believe me. Is this the turning, I can't see the road sign?'

'I think so.'

The cottage hospital was a one-storey structure of unprepossessing appearance which had so far managed to escape the various bureaucratic lunacies inflicted on the rest of the Health Service and rendered stalwart service to the local community. Originally opened by and named after a minor member of the Royal family during the reign of Edward VII, it had scarcely changed over the years and inside resembled a somewhat dilapidated country house rather than an institution. There had always been a refreshing lack of red tape, strict visiting hours were ignored and the staff were casually efficient.

Tony and Martin slid up the incline to the front entrance and found the foyer decorated with home-made paper-chains in fine disregard of fire precautions. A collection of Christmas cards had been pinned on the notice board behind the reception desk together with a rude cartoon of one of the doctors depicted as a Fairy Godmother waving what appeared to be a catheter as a wand.

'We've come to see my father,' Tony said. 'Mr Chivers. He was admitted yesterday.'

The receptionist looked at her list. 'Oh, yes, he's in the Armitage Ward. Have a word with the staff nurse before you go in. Down there and first left.'

'Why do hospitals always smell funny?' Martin whispered.

'Mr Chivers?' the staff nurse said when they reached her station. 'He's quite a character, your father. The doctor's had a look at him this morning and thinks we ought to keep him in a bit longer.'

'He's not worse, though?'

'No, no. Had a disturbed night, but that was to be expected. His temperature's down, so I'm sure he'll be home in a day or two. Do go in.'

They went into the small ward holding four beds, only three of which were occupied. There was a skinhead propped up in the one nearest the door; he had a dressing over one eye and his whole face was swollen and purple. The third occupant was a very old man who appeared to be asleep. There were more paper-chains, some of which had sagged and were hanging down like coloured sausages.

'How are you feeling, Pop?' Tony said.

'Very fair, love.' His eyes were paler than usual and watery.

'Looking after you, are they?'

'Oh, yes.'

'And the doctor's pleased with you, I gather.'

'Said I was a wonder for my age.'

'What's the food like, Pop?' Martin asked.

'They bring you a menu, you can choose.'

'Can you? That's good. Did you have Christmas lunch?'

'Very good. But no custard. I told the nurse they should have served custard with the pudding.'

'How's the ankle feel now?' Tony said.

'He's very satisfied with me, the doctor. Very satisfied.'

The old man in the third bed had a face like parchment. Now, as they looked, he suddenly made a disturbing wheezing noise as he expelled a breath.

'Chummy there's on his way out if you ask me,' Pop said, in a whisper too loud for comfort. 'They put the screens round him earlier and I thought, hello, he's a gonner.'

Tony saw the other old man's eyes flicker and thought it best to change the subject. 'Well, let's hope not.' But his father was anxious to impart as much bad news as possible. 'The woman who brings the tea round in the morning said they'd had one go in the night. Not in this ward, one of the women.'

Will I be as sanguine about death at his age? Tony thought. Does the fear recede as one gets closer?

'She's coloured, of course, the tea lady, and how's everything at home? Expect you missed me.'

'Yes, yes, we did.'

'Did you play whist?'

'No, Pop.'

'Oh, pity, pity. We always played whist at Christmas.'

'We had a quiet evening, not only because of you but Jenny had a bit of bad news . . . Andy's been injured in a bomb explosion.'

His father stared at him, silenced at last.

'The IRA blew up one of his vehicles, but he wasn't inside it at the time, so happily he didn't get seriously hurt. Just concussed.'

'Oh, dear. Oh dear.'

'Jenny felt she had to go to him, so she flew to Belfast yesterday.' The face he watched was suddenly transformed by an inarticulate rage: teeth clenched, the words hissed out. 'Course I know what I'd do with them if I was in charge, I'd kill the lot of them.' Anger contorted his whole body. 'No trial, nothing. The moment they were caught they'd be put up against a wall and shot.'

'Yes, the problem is catching them, Pop . . . Anyway, I thought you ought to know.'

'That's bad news, bad news, not what we expected.'

'Sister says they'd like to keep you in a little longer. Is there anything you want?'

'No, thanks, thanks all the same. I've got the telly, going to watch the football later. Well, give her my love. I didn't want to hear that, that was the last thing I wanted to hear.'

'Kate will be in this evening. Would you like her to bring you some fruit or cake?'

'Wouldn't mind my new dressing gown. The one they give you doesn't go round me.'

'Dressing gown, right, I'll remember.' He bent and kissed his father's forehead. 'Take care of yourself, don't flirt with the nurses.'

'I give them a laugh, I do. They're good sports.'

'I bet. Have to be with you around.'

Tony smiled at the skinhead on the way out, but got no response.

'I expect Pop will have to stay with you when he comes out,' Martin said.

'Yes,' Tony said as the same thought struck him and he examined his feelings.

'He looked smaller than usual. As if he'd shrunk suddenly.'

'Most people do when they get older.'

They bought some milk at the garage and filled up with petrol. Then, after driving a short distance, Tony pulled into a side street and stopped. He left the engine running to keep the heater on.

'I want to tell you something before we discuss you,' he began, 'something about what happened to me once.' He opened his side window a few inches and lit a cigarette. 'I'm going to give up in the New Year.'

'Again?'

'Well, I'm going to try . . . You see,' beginning again,

145

'you're not the only one to get into this situation. I did the same thing once, before I met your mother.'

'You?' Martin said, unable to keep the surprise out of his voice.

'When I was roughly the same age as you, maybe a touch older, I had a serious affair with a girl called Joyce – Joyce Hunter,' Tony said, gratified that he could still recall her surname from across the years. 'We got as far as planning to marry as soon as I'd saved enough. Then she discovered she was pregnant ... and of course then abortion was illegal, a criminal offence in certain circumstances, you could go to jail ... though of course if you had the money there were ways around it. Otherwise you took your chances with some old woman in a back street. That was very dicey, dangerous ... but there it was, if you were desperate enough it was often the only way. That or get the girl to take a hot bath, drink a whole bottle of gin and then go for a ride on a bus.'

'On a bus?'

'It was an old wives' tale that sometimes worked I gather. Mind you, I'd give birth if I drank a whole bottle of gin.'

'Did you try that?'

'No, but we tried everything else we could think of. A little knowledge in those days was certainly a dangerous thing. We were too scared to ask our parents, we had to rely on friends who were as ignorant as we were. Nothing we did had any effect and by then she was nearly three months gone. Then somebody told us to go to a bent trick cyclist.'

'What's that mean?' Martin interrupted.

'Psychiatrist, haven't you heard them called that before? There were quite a few amenable ones around if you knew where to find them. For a price they were prepared to certify that the girl was not in a fit mental state to go through with it. Allegedly that got around the law, still dodgy, but these characters got away with it in most cases, plus getting rich in the process. Once you got that far, they also gave you the address of a private clinic where an equally shady doctor would do the actual abortion. They were clinics in name only, usually just a fairly primitive operating room in an ordinary house. The going rate was a hundred quid minimum, which I suppose would be the equivalent of a thousand today . . . Strictly cash, of course, they didn't want any records kept . . . I can't remember exactly how I came up with the money, I think I pawned my watch and she had a bit in her post office account . . . Somehow we managed to scrape up what they were asking . . . I took her to the place . . . just off the Marylebone Road, but I wasn't allowed to go in with her, I had to leave her there. They told me to come back in an hour. That was a very long hour, believe me. They didn't actually finish it there, you see, they just induced it with something, some injection I suppose.'

'Why couldn't they do the whole thing there?'

'Too much of a risk . . . If anything went wrong they didn't want it going wrong on their premises. Anyway, when she came out I got a taxi and we went to her girlfriend's flat to wait. They'd told her it would start happening in about an hour. They got that right. She started screaming exactly an hour later.'

He paused and wound the window down further, flicking his spent cigarette into a pile of snow.

'I was terrified, of course, terrified she was going to bleed to death . . . I never imagined . . . well, I don't know what I imagined, certainly nothing like it was . . . but between us, me and the girlfriend that is, we somehow managed to get Joyce through it, and afterwards . . . well, I don't want to go into the rest . . . when the worst was over we called the friend's doctor and said she'd had a miscarriage. He knew what had really happened, of course, but he turned a blind eye and took care of her.'

'Christ,' Martin said finally.

'Anyway, the whole point of telling you that was not to frighten you . . . but that, afterwards, Joyce never wanted to see me again. Understandably. We'd not only killed the baby, we'd killed whatever we felt for each other. I had nothing but guilt and she just couldn't bear to have me around reminding her. It was over.' As he finished it occurred to him that he had never told anybody the story, not even Kate. It was funny how life was divided between the right things you did and the wrong things. He couldn't remember Joyce's face any more, only the hurt.

'Christ,' Martin said again. 'But it's not like that now, is it? There are proper places where it's done properly, aren't there?'

'Yes, it's all different now, that part of it, thank God. The only thing that isn't different is the human factor. I don't know what you really feel for Patricia, but forty-eight hours ago you told me you and she were washed up. Now, obviously, the situation has changed, so the only advice I can give you is for both of you to think very carefully before you decide one way or the other. It's not like buying or selling a car.'

'I know that. Don't think I don't. Even before you told me what happened to you.' He fiddled with the glove compartment.

'Have you rung her since she called you?' Martin shook his head. 'Are you going to?'

'I daren't ring her home.'

'Well, is there somewhere you can meet and talk about it calmly?'

'I could go to Deborah's.'

'Who's Deborah?'

'Her best friend.'

'Do you have Deborah's number?'

'Yes.'

'Then, get her to ring Patricia, wouldn't that be a good idea?'

'Yes, I suppose so . . . It's all such a bloody mess.'

'Well, when we get home make that phone call. You have to see her again, it won't just go away. And whatever you both decide, I'll do what I can.' Tony slipped the handbrake off. 'We'd better get back, don't want your mother thinking we've had an accident.'

They were nearly at the house before Martin spoke again. 'I'm glad you told me that story,' he said, looking straight ahead. 'I never thought of things like that happening to you.'

'Just between you and me,' Tony said.

Ten

'This is the only one of yours I haven't read,' Harvey said as he took a copy down from the shelves. 'The moment Jenny told me you were her father, I went out and got the others.'

They were in Tony's study following a subdued lunch – the previous dramas seemed to have drained them of everything but small-talk; that and the sense of anticlimax that always settles on Boxing Day.

'It's difficult to get hold of,' Tony explained. 'Been out of print for years, and they only did a small edition. First novels seldom make it. But borrow it.'

'Can I? I'm very good with books, I promise you, I always return them. This was your first, you say?'

'Not quite. The first to be accepted. I wrote at least three turgid epics before that saw the light of day. It's thinly veiled autobiography of course. Sacred and profane bits of my misspent youth are scattered in those pages. I haven't looked at it in years.'

'Is that true of every writer when he writes his first book?'

'Who knows? I suspect so, if they're honest, which most of us aren't.'

'What gave you the title?'

'*Mumbled Prayers*? I can't remember. A none too subtle hint I suspect. I was doubtless praying somebody would take it.'

They were joined by Kate and Bill.

'We ought to get the show on the road,' Bill said. 'Otherwise it's going to be a remake of *The Man Who Came to Dinner*. The *men* in our case.'

'Did either of you ever read that wonderful story by Stephen Leacock?' They shook their heads. 'I've got it here somewhere. It was about a curate who was so pathologically polite he could never bring himself to get up and leave. He came for tea and stayed until he died.'

'Oh, well done, Tony. He's known as Mr Tact,' Kate said.

'No, Bill's right, we really ought to be going. Are the others around? Must say goodbye.'

'Evelyn and Martin have gone for a walk, and Roger's not back yet.'

'Well please say goodbye to them all for us.'

'You really have to go now?'

'Yes, I have to prepare a presentation for a

breakfast meeting tomorrow and I haven't even started yet.'

'A breakfast meeting, my God! Imagine what I'd be like,' Tony said.

'And listen,' Bill said, 'in the New Year let's shake faces at each other. I hope you'll both come up to London and let us return the hospitality. Sample some old Southern cooking.'

'I accept,' Kate said. 'When?'

'You've got our number, so give us a bell tonight and we'll compare diaries. And be sure and let us know the latest on Andy.'

'Let's you and me put our feet up in front of the fire for half an hour,' Kate said when the two Americans had driven away. 'We deserve it. Besides I want to know how you got on with Martin. You did have your talk, didn't you?'

'Yes, we got around to it.'

Tony put another log on the fire, and pulled the two armchairs closer.

'How did he take it, was he upset?'

'Yes. But I think I got through to him.'

'He looked a bit shaken when he got in. How did you put it? Darling, don't smoke. How many have you had today?'

'Not many. Don't get at me, please. I'll just have this one.'

'That might be the one that kills you.'

'No, I smoked that one a long time ago. When I was fourteen. Do you want to know what happened with Martin or not?'

'I'm only thinking of you.'

'I know, I know,' he said. It was a dialogue they had most days. 'I'll quit when I've finished this next book.'

'You said that last time.'

He took one drag and threw the cigarette into the fire. It missed and bounced back onto the carpet.

'Now look what you've done.'

'Didn't burn, didn't burn,' he said, picking it up and succeeding the second time. 'Well, obviously I rammed home the pros and cons of an abortion, but I think what really terrifies him is her parents. Mind you, I remembered how I felt when I had to face yours for the first time. They didn't approve of me, remember?'

'My mother adored you.'

'When I'd charmed her, maybe. Your father was going to kill me at one point.'

'That was just his way.'

'Darling, I don't want to speak ill of the dead, but your father was out of the Dark Ages. However, don't let's go back into history, let's stick to Martin. What he's going to do is meet Patricia on neutral ground – apparently her best friend has a place they can use. Or they could meet here for that matter, if the friend doesn't work out.'

'You didn't suggest that, did you? I don't think I could cope with an emotional pregnant teenager right now.'

'I didn't mean to stay, just come here.'

'Not even come here.'

'No, okay, you're right, that's not a good idea. Better they work it out for themselves.'

'It's all so clinical,' Kate said, staring into the fire.

'Do you have any better ideas?'

'If it was Jenny I'd know exactly how to deal with it, but I can't get near Martin. He's so secretive.'

'We were the same. The day after your father told you never to see me again we were in bed together.'

Kate kicked her shoes off and massaged her toes.

'Admit it,' Tony said. He smiled at her, trying to get her to see the funny side of it, but she was not to be coerced.

'Yes. Funnily enough I talked about that to Evelyn last night. Jenny tells me everything.'

'Now she may do. But you forget we went through more or less the same thing with her. There was a time when you and she fought like cats. How many sleepless nights did we have when she was going out with that chinless wonder – what was his name? – Bertram?'

'Brindsley. Anyway she made the right choice in the end. Andy's perfect for her.'

'Exactly. And we had no hand in it. Likewise Martin. If he fucks it up, which by the law of averages he probably will, then all we can do is be here to pick up the pieces.'

Kate stared into the fire for a long time. 'At first,' she said finally, 'when they're tiny, you never think this far ahead. You imagine that once they've grown up and maybe moved away, all your troubles are over. It's the mistake all mothers make. You don't have a baby, you have something that's with you for life.' Her thoughts grew sad and envious. 'It must be comforting to be like Patricia's parents, to have a faith that decides everything for you so that you never have to think twice.'

'I guess something like that must have turned Roger in the direction of Mecca,' Tony said.

'Yes, I suppose so.' She switched topics abruptly. 'And, that reminds me, I still haven't rung Vanessa to tell her about the children's presents. They'll think we've forgotten them. Where're you going?' she ended as Tony got up and started for the door.

'You saying that about Vanessa reminded me of something else. I must make a note that Harvey borrowed one of my books. People always say they're going to return them and they never do. I don't want to lose this one, it's my only copy.'

Left alone Kate allowed herself to be mesmerised by the flames. She yearned to get clear of the tangle of their lives, to see the way ahead. She could see herself gradually vegetating like some of the earnest women she encountered shopping in the village, with their talk of coffee mornings, the latest hairdresser, where they had their nails done, holidays in their second home on the Costa Brava, which plastic surgeon did the best face job – all the trivia of affluence that repelled her.

Eleven

'A girl was murdered in these woods last year,' Martin said. He reached for Evelyn's hand and helped her over a small patch of ice. The trees, mostly conifers, were so close together that there was only a sprinkling of snow beneath their straight trunks. A few years back, playing here with friends, he had had no difficulty imagining mounted Cossacks hidden in the dark recesses of a forest – an image carried away from several visits to the reissue of *Dr Zhivago*, the first film to awaken his longing to experience romantic love with somebody as disturbing as Julie Christie. Now he saw the forest of his tumescent dreams for what it really was – a few acres of uncared-for woodland, devastated by the two great storms; fallen trees rotted by the paths, the smaller branches denuded of bark, whitened like human limbs that had never seen the sun. Ground ivy had clawed its way over the jagged stumps, and elsewhere termites had begun the gradual process of crumbling away the trees' remains. In places the blasted trunks stood branchless, holed by birds, and, as he and Evelyn picked their way along a narrow path, a robin kept pace close at hand, now flying ahead of them, now waiting.

'They never found who did it,' he continued, 'though they arrested one man, somebody local, related to the girl, but in the end they couldn't prove anything and let him go. I think it was somewhere over there they found her.'

'Well, don't show me.'

'No, I wasn't going to,' he said hastily. Waiting at the back of his mind were the thoughts he needed to share with her, but he could not find the key to unlock them. Mention of the murdered girl had evoked darker pictures: the story his father had told him had become his own, with Patricia as the victim. It was difficult for him to imagine his father as a young man, involved like himself, but the story he had been told haunted him. Image after image moved through his imagination like one of those trick packs of picture cards that you flicked to make the characters jerk into a parody of life. His camera eye focused on a girl, foetal-folded on a bed, screaming, waiting for the end of something; his father, the perpetrator, watching, helpless. He forced his mind to blur what came next, turning abruptly to save Evelyn falling as she stumbled on a tree root. 'I did tell you, didn't I?' he began, relinquishing his hold on her arm, 'that Patricia called me?'

'Yes.'

'Christmas Eve,' he said as though the actual day somehow bestowed a special significance. Then he faltered again. 'She . . . had a particular reason for ringing me . . . something I've been meaning to tell you ever since.'

'Perhaps I can guess,' Evelyn replied.

'Can you?' he blurted.

'Well, I'm quite good at reading other people. I knew you were upset about something.'

'It's nothing you've done, don't think that. Just my own stupid, bloody fault . . . ' He felt rescued by the straw she had given him. 'It's just that, before I met you, Pat and I were very thick . . . well, I never pretended otherwise, did I? She wouldn't accept that I could be seeing her and you at the same time. She became more and more jealous and we had awful rows about it, ending with her saying she never wanted to see me again.'

'And now she's changed her mind, is that it?'

'Yes and no, it's not as simple as that,' he said miserably. 'I wish it was.'

His resolve failed him at that point, and Evelyn took over. 'Martin, don't take what I'm going to say the wrong way, but if it makes it any easier for you, you mustn't think that I've read anything more into our relationship than just friendship. That's not to say I haven't enjoyed the times we've spent together, because I have and I hope we'll always remain friends . . . The fact that I've been able to meet your parents and spend Christmas with you all was something special. But if what you're trying to tell me is that your feelings for Patricia haven't really changed, then don't worry any more on my account. I understand.'

Rather than bring comfort, what she said now added an extra layer of remorse: her anger would have been more welcome. He stopped walking, crunching thin sheet ice beneath his feet as he turned to look straight at her for the first time. Weak sunlight filtered between the trees; the robin, disturbed by Martin's sudden movement, flashed through a shaft.

'She thinks she's pregnant,' he said, 'that's what she rang to tell me.' He searched Evelyn's face for her reaction, expecting the revelation to produce some violent change in her, but it was not forthcoming. For a moment he thought she hadn't taken it in and that the effort it had cost him actually to confess had been wasted. Then she said, 'Well, I didn't have to be psychic to realise it must have been something like that.'

'I've been dreading telling you.' In his relief, he became cruel, not deliberately so, but in the way young people do when all their emotions are centred upon themselves. 'If she is, and wants to have it, I think, and I've thought about it very seriously – well, I've thought about nothing else really – then I want to do the right thing and marry her, if that's what she wants.'

How young he is, she thought, too young for me. Why did I ever allow myself to be here? What a fool you are, what a fool. And how old-fashioned the phrase he used – 'the right thing' – like something out of a Victorian novel. His face, like his concerns, was naked, none of her own pain was etched on it.

'Of course you must,' she said.

'After all, getting rid of a child isn't like buying or selling a car, is it?'

'No.'

'I mean, it can be very dangerous, can't it?' His father's story edged back into his consciousness together with half-remembered smatterings of biology – the gestation process, the size of the foetus at given moments in its development, when it became a person somewhere along the line – the little knowledge inextricably implanted into Patricia's naked body once so undefiled.

Now it was Evelyn's turn to search for the right words. 'But it hasn't come to that yet, has it? From what you say, it's only a possibility . . . Has she missed her periods?'

'Yes.'

'How many?'

'Two.'

'Does she ever miss one occasionally?'

'I don't really know. Is that usual?'

'Well it's not unknown. Lots of things can cause it, none of them to do with pregnancy.'

'Really?'

'Sure. You could both be worrying for nothing.'

'What sort of things?'

'Oh, not eating – she's not anorexic, is she?'

'I don't think so, except she's always going on about what she can and can't eat.'

'Well, I'm sure she's not, you'd have noticed. Even a cold can sometimes stop it . . . D'you want to marry her? Or put it another way, if this hadn't come up, would you still?'

At that moment a couple walking their dog came into view. Martin and Evelyn stepped to either side of the path to let them pass. The dog, a long-haired retriever, its muzzle speckled with snow, paused and regarded them before it was called to heel by its owners who, in a very British way, affected to ignore that there was anybody else on the path, convincing Martin that his guilty secret was apparent even to total strangers. The previous mood broken, he and Evelyn resumed their stroll. He felt grateful that the interruption had prevented him from answering her last question, although his mind was now made up. They walked on in silence, like strangers who had briefly shared part of a journey, as powdery snow dropped weightlessly from the trees.

Twelve

Roger returned just as Kate was leaving to visit Pop. She stopped their old Volvo alongside Roger's more recent model and wound down her window. 'How did the meeting go?'

'Fine.'

'I'm just off to the hospital.'

'Oh. Be sure and give Pop my best.'

As Roger went into the house through the garage, Emily jumped down from a pile of packing cases where she often slept and squeezed ahead of him. She started to purr the moment they were both inside, excited that she had outwitted a stranger, and followed him to Tony's study.

'Is she allowed to stay in?' he asked his brother.

'Yes. Let her for once.' Tony picked up the cat and the purr became a growl. 'But be good, just sit in front of the fire and behave like a normal cat.' He plonked her down and Emily stared up at him, her mind working out the odds against doing as she was told or going walkabout.

'You were up and away early,' Tony said.

'Yes.'

'Business meeting I gather?'

'Not exactly.' Roger sat in the fireside armchair and warmed his hands. 'I've thought a lot more about what we said to each other last night. I can see why you thought I was joking.'

'I never said that.'

'When I first arrived, I mean. You were very flippant.'

'That's just my way. You took me by surprise. No Vanessa, no kids, being on the wagon, taking up your new religion, it was quite a shopping list to take on board.'

'Yes. Plus the fact that I didn't tell you all.'

'There's more?' Tony said.

'In a sense. More explanation I should have said . . . The meeting I went to this morning, that was AA. There's a chapter fairly locally, you're never very far away from one. I attend most days, sometimes when it's bad I go twice a day.'

'And it helps?'

'Oh, yes. It certainly helps to know you're not alone.'

'How long have you been going?'

'Just over three months. Thirteen weeks next Wednesday to be exact.' He looked at Tony and gave a wan smile. 'You take it one day at a time.'

'What decided you?'

Emily suddenly sprang up onto Roger's lap and began to knead her front paws into his thighs.

'Sling her off,' Tony said. 'She's a nightmare that animal. Especially when she starts making bread. Remember how mother used to call it that?'

'Yes,' Roger said. 'Yes, I do. Old Tiger, wasn't that his name?'

'Tiger,' Tony said. 'Fancy you remembering that.'

'I remember a lot,' Roger said. 'Being on your own concentrates the mind.'

'You started to tell me . . . ' Tony reminded him.

'I was in the office attending one of the partners' weekly meetings and I looked around the Board table at the other partners, looked at them as though for the first time, and they suddenly seemed like people from another planet, spending their lives finding ways around the tax laws to make rich people richer. And I thought, I'm no different, I'm going to be here until I'm sixty and they'll give me the farewell dinner and the inscribed silver tray, and I'll have done nothing with my life . . . D'you know what I'm talking about?'

'We all have those moments,' Tony said.

'I stopped listening to what they were saying, almost as if I was floating above them, disembodied. I knew that I had to clear the decks before it was too late. Start over.'

'Did it have to be so drastic?'

'Meaning leaving Vanessa?'

'Yes, that,' Tony said. 'But I was thinking more about the religion. I can understand a marriage going wrong, and obviously Kate and I are sad that you and Vanessa can't make a go of it . . . but, without being flippant again, the religious bit doesn't seem to add up with the rest.'

Roger took his time before answering. Emily had settled down by now, folded like a sphinx, staring fixedly into the fire. 'Yes, I can see why you think that . . . but you've no idea how empty my life was . . . I was suffocating. What happened was, what changed it all . . . It started when I was in Manchester on a business trip seeing an important client. I was in charge of the account – I'd made a pig's ear of it, forgotten to lodge an appeal on the due date and cost the client two hundred thousand. He was furious and fired me. That night I went on a blinder, a real blinder. Woke up the next morning in a strange bedroom with a whore . . . and couldn't remember anything, how I'd got there, what else I'd done . . . That was the moment I realised I wasn't just a heavy drinker, I was an alcoholic. That same morning I went to AA and said, "save me." You have to admit it before they'll take you on.'

'Jesus,' Tony said as Roger finished. 'If only you'd told me before, I might have been able to help.'

Roger shook his head. 'I doubt it. I was too far down

the line – cunning, secretive – drunks are you know. I had drink hidden all over the place . . . Vodka, because that's easier to conceal, you can't detect it on the breath like whisky or gin. And, of course, if Vanessa challenged me, I lied. I lied to everybody, including myself. I was expert at it. I did things which now make me go cold.'

'Like what, for instance?'

'Driving home without knowing how I got there. How I didn't kill anybody is a miracle. I was lucky, if you can call it luck . . . The thing about AA is that everybody in it has travelled the same road, faced the same nightmares. You help each other, there's always somebody at the end of a phone when the pressures build up again, as they do . . . There's no permanent cure, you're always in holding pattern. My main contact happens to be an Iranian.'

'Iranian?'

'Yes. A man, about my age, who came to England in the Diplomatic Corps while the Shah was still in power. When the revolution happened and the Shah was deposed, he was trapped here, for a time in fear of his life I gather. His family was still in Iran but he couldn't return and they couldn't get out. That's how it started for him. The more I got to know him, the more I was impressed by his calmness . . . he told me that what gave him the strength to go on was his total belief, his faith. He showed me . . . me who never believed in anything, certainly not the religion I was confirmed in . . . that there is something beyond the evidence . . . and the long and the short of it is,' Roger concluded, 'he converted me.' He looked at Tony and shrugged. 'I don't blame you for thinking it a bit of a joke, I suppose it must still seem that way.'

'What's Vanessa's attitude?'

'Ah!' Roger said, 'Well, it's still a sick joke with her. Not going to AA, she welcomed that, but the conversion. We've had frightful rows about it, long bruising rows when we both said things not easily forgotten or forgiven. In the end it became poisonous for the children, so I moved out. I've been living in a motel for the past two months.'

'Well, thank God you came here for Christmas,' Tony said.

'It took an effort, but the truth is it was the one time I couldn't face being on my own. So, now you know the whole story.'

'I guess it creeps up on you without you noticing.' He wanted to show Roger that he really did understand at last. 'The odd social drink which becomes the second and then the third. I know I drink too much on occasions, and I certainly smoke too much.'

'Smoking doesn't destroy marriages.'

'Well . . . I get a lot of stick from Kate. D'you think you and Vanessa can ever repair it?'

'Maybe. Perhaps if she believes I've licked the drink

she'll come round to the other.' He stroked the cat and she arched her back, luxuriating.

'I envy you having a faith, I never have.'

'That's the first time I can ever remember you envying me about anything,' Roger said.

Thirteen

Ted Turner was at her father-in-law's bedside when Kate arrived.

'I've brought you your dressing gown, Pop,' she said. 'And some fruit and mince pies.'

'Very nice, love. Very nice. Put them there, I'll have them later.'

'That's very smart,' Ted said, admiring the gown.

'They chose it for me special.'

'How're you feeling, dear?'

'He's coming along,' Ted answered for him, but there was a certain reservation in his voice which Kate was quick to detect. 'He gave himself a nasty jolt, but I think he's on the mend.'

They both stayed chatting with the old man for ten minutes, but he seemed disinclined to take part and several times his eyes closed. Looking around Kate saw that only one other bed was occupied – a shaven-headed youth who was listening to a Walkman.

'You feeling sleepy? They wake you up so early in hospitals, don't they?'

Pop's eyes stayed closed and Kate exchanged a look with Ted. 'Well, one of us will come in again tomorrow. Nothing we can bring you?'

This time she got a response. 'Have you heard any more about Andy?'

'Yes, I spoke to Jenny and he's off the critical list.'

'Good. That's what we want to hear, love.' His eyes closed again. She bent over the bed and kissed him. 'You take care of yourself. Least you're nice and warm in here. It's bitter outside.'

On the way out to the frozen car park she said: 'How is he really?'

'Well, they're watching the old ticker, that's a bit weak. I've told them to change the medication because he's getting a reaction from the antibiotic.'

'But nothing to worry about?'

'Not really, except he's not responding as quickly as I thought. How old is he now?'

'Eighty-three, I think.'

'Well, any fall at that age is dicey. I'll look at him again first thing. Does he live on his own?'

'Yes, more or less. He has a woman come in and tidy up a couple of days a week. But he can come back to us when he gets out.'

Although she had given the undertaking automatically, she hated herself for the uncharitable thoughts that immediately entered her mind as she

173

drove home. She remembered her own mother being chained to the house for years looking after an invalid sister, who, in the end, ironically, outlived her. She suddenly saw the same future stretching ahead for her. It wasn't that she didn't like him, or feel sorry for him, but right at that moment she was more sorry for herself.

She arrived back to find the other four waiting for a repeat of an old *Morecambe and Wise* show to start.

'Ted was already with him when I got there,' she reported. 'He's a bit concerned about Pop's heart. So they're not letting him out just yet.'

'When he says "concerned"?'

'Because of his age.'

'I'll go in early tomorrow.'

Kate welcomed the programme starting; she needed some comedy for a change and found she had forgotten how uniquely British Morecambe and Wise had been, their humour gentle – Morecambe, with the baffled expressions and exquisite timing, Wise, the cocky one, their exchanges dovetailing perfectly, both of them so refreshingly different from the current crop dishing out something called 'alternative comedy'.

'Oh, I do miss them, ' she said when it was over. 'And tell me something, what is alternative comedy? It's either comedy or it isn't, and to me it isn't. Or is that just me?'

'I'm not mad about it either,' Evelyn commented.

'Started with Lenny Bruce,' Tony said. 'Way back. Remember his Pope routine? That killed me the first time I heard it. Because what he did, and nobody had done it before, was to destroy all the icons. Imagine saying to the Pope, "Nobody knows you're Jewish, baby." '

'Yes, he was brilliant,' Kate agreed. 'You couldn't believe what you were hearing, it was so dangerous, you felt you were part of a revolution.'

'Too bad he blew his brains out with coke,' Tony said. 'Nobody before him had had the nerve to go that far. He took on the politicians, brought them down to our level. Nobody did character assassination on politicians before that. He was Oswald with a verbal bullet.'

They all spent the next half an hour discussing their respective favourites, and for the first time since Christmas Eve Kate was able to forget the various family dramas and enjoy herself.

'They say most jokes originate in the Stock Exchange or banks,' Roger observed. 'D'you think that's true?'

'The Stock Exchange is a joke in itself,' Tony said. 'Equally, most jokes are ethnic, a sort of socially acceptable racism.'

'What about your faculty?' Kate asked Evelyn. 'Are they a jokey lot?'

'Not very. Stuffy bunch most of them, but then they lead such cloistered, pampered lives, they're too wrapped up in themselves to stoop to humour.'

'How about you, Martin?' Roger asked. 'What sort of jokes are going the rounds in Oxford?' And Kate thought, he's suddenly come to life, he's no longer on the defensive and edgy.

'You really want to hear one?'

'Yes, give us an example.'

'Well, a man goes to his doctor who says "I've got some bad news for you, and some worse news." So the man says, "Okay give me the bad news first." "You've got Aids," the doctor says. "Oh, no!" the man says. "What's the worse news then?" "You've also got Alzheimer's." And the man says, "Oh, thank God I haven't got Aids." '

He laughed and both Tony and Evelyn joined in, while Roger grimaced and Kate said: 'But that's an awful joke, Martin. Sick. I'm going to make some coffee. Or tea. I can make both. Which would you like, Evelyn?'

'I think tea for a change. I drink too much coffee.'

'I'll help you,' Martin volunteered.

'Oh, wonders will never cease.'

He followed his mother into the kitchen saying, 'If you think that's sick you should hear some of them.'

'No thank you.'

Judging the moment opportune he busied himself with the cups and saucers and said chirpily, 'Mum, I thought I'd push off tomorrow.'

'Tomorrow?' She stopped what she was doing. 'I thought you were going to stay until New Year?'

'Yes, I was, but something's come up.'

'What?'

He avoided her eyes. 'I've arranged to see Patricia.'

'I see. What about Evelyn? You invited her here, you can't up and leave her, that would be very rude.'

'Oh, she doesn't mind. We talked about it this afternoon.'

'And is she leaving too?'

'Yes. I'll drive her back to her place first, then go on.'

'What have you decided about Pat?' She tried to make it sound casual.

'Decided? . . . Nothing yet.'

'You must have some idea.'

'Yes, course I do, but I haven't spoken to her yet.'

'I thought you said you had.' Still casual.

'No, I phoned her friend and we're meeting at the friend's flat.'

'You know what's always been your trouble, Martin? You rush into everything without stopping to think. That joke you told in there. Aids isn't a joke, people die from it, it's a death warrant.'

'I know that.'

'You say that and yet you obviously didn't take

177

precautions with Pat, otherwise you wouldn't be in the situation you're in.'

'We did, it just didn't work that's all.'

'What about the other girls you've slept with? It only takes one.'

'They're not those sort of girls.'

'That's what everybody says until it happens.'

'I haven't been with anybody else but Pat for the past six months, so I don't know what you're worrying about. Not on that score anyway.'

'A thing like this could ruin your whole life.' She pressed home the plunger on the cafetière.

'Not necessarily . . . Just because you've forgotten what it's like.'

'What's that meant to mean?'

'Being in love. I bet you and Daddy weren't always careful.'

The kitchen door closed behind him and she heard him go upstairs. A memory of him as a child returned; she remembered waking up in the middle of the night with a mother's intuition that something was wrong and going into his bedroom, fearful of another illness after the meningitis scare, to reassure herself. She had found him crying. 'Why is it,' he had asked her, 'that the good things don't last and all the bad things go on and on?' One of those unanswerable questions that children throw at you. She relived that moment now, thinking, why don't I understand him more? Perhaps he's right, perhaps I have forgotten what it is like, that peculiar pain, buried in the heart, you can never share with anyone else.

Fourteen

Tony waited for the cry to be repeated, uncertain as to what had woken him. He sat up in bed cautiously, careful not to disturb Kate. Never mind Pop's heart, he thought, as his own hammered away. The week before Christmas he had been visited by the local community policeman and cautioned to be extra vigilant over the holiday period. 'Don't worry about calling us out if you hear or see anything suspicious. We'd rather be wrong than sorry.'

He strained forward in the bed, concentrating. There were the usual house noises – water suddenly burbling in the pipes, the clunks from somewhere down below – but he was convinced that he had heard a human scream. Was the alarm on, the cat outside? The fact that the police had told him the majority of break-ins occurred during the daylight hours was cold comfort.

He was just about to relax when the scream came

again. He judged it to be at the bottom of the garden. Definitely human. A girl being attacked, raped. He reached across Kate for the phone, knocking it off the hook. He half fell out of bed and crawled his way to the other side, groping around until he had grasped the swinging instrument. He punched in 999.

A calm operator's voice answered. 'Emergency service. Which d'you require please?'

'Police.'

'Where are you ringing from, sir?'

Tony had a momentary black-out before remembering their number.

'Your name, sir?'

'Chivers. Tony Chivers.'

'Is that a private number you're calling from, sir?'

'Yes, my home, please hurry, it's urgent.'

'Can you give me the address, sir?'

Tony gave it.

'Stay on the line, please.'

While he waited he heard the scream a third time. It seemed nearer if anything. Christ! he thought, she's being murdered in our garden. Kate stirred.

'What is it? What're you doing?'

'Shh! Come on, come on,' he urged into the phone.

'Slough police,' a male voice said.

'Oh, thank God! Somebody's being attacked in our garden, sounds like a girl. I heard the screams.'

'Is that Mr Chivers talking?'

'Yes.'

'Right, Mr Chivers, we'll get somebody there as soon as possible. Don't go outside yourself.'

By now Kate was bleary but awake. She reached to turn on the light.

'Don't!' Tony hissed, putting his hand over hers. 'There's a girl being murdered or raped in the garden. I heard the screams, that's what woke me. I've rung the police, they're on their way.'

'I didn't hear the alarm go off.'

'Well, the alarm hasn't gone off. It only goes off if somebody gets inside.'

The next scream froze them both. 'Oh, God,' she whispered, 'it's right under the window. Don't go and look, stay here.'

'I must do something. Maybe if I shouted he'd stop.'

'Tony, if you go outside I'll never forgive you. Wait until the police come.'

'But she could be dead by then.'

'So could you. Don't do anything, please. Stay here.'

They waited.

'Can you hear anything?'

'No.'

'Did the police say how long they'd take?'

'Just that they were on their way. Depends where they were of course.'

'We should have had those lights put in at the back, I told you.'

'Yes, I will now, I'll do something about them as soon as the shops open again.' They were both still whispering.

'Hand me my dressing gown,' Kate said.

'Where is it?'

'On the foot of the bed.'

He reached back without changing his position and handed it to her. She wrapped it around her shoulders.

'How will we know when they get here?'

'We'll see their headlights.'

'So will he. Why do they have to have their lights on?'

'They have to see where they're going.'

'Can you hear anything now? Listen. Is that some-body trying the french windows?'

'What did you hear?'

'Sounded like he was trying the catch.'

'I didn't hear anything.'

'Don't talk.'

'You're talking.'

Kate knelt on the bed, her head cocked to one side as she listened intently. 'There's definitely somebody there,' she whispered.

'I wish I had a gun,' Tony said.

'They'd arrest you if you had.'

'I think I heard a car.' He crawled around the end of the bed, making his way towards the window.

'Tony, don't.'

'I'm only going to peek to make sure.'

He edged the rest of the distance to the window on his stomach, then slowly raised himself to sill height and eased the drawn curtains aside a fraction.

'Yes, the police are here,' he whispered back to her. 'I can see their torches.' He got to his feet, suddenly released from abject cowardice. 'I'd better go down and turn the alarm off.'

'Turn it off?'

'Well I have to be able to let the police in, don't I?'

'Supposing it's not the police.'

'Course it's the police.'

'Sometimes criminals impersonate them. I read of a case only the other day.'

'Don't be ridiculous. I rang them. Why else would they be here?'

He staggered to the door. 'Oh, shit! Bollocks!'

'What have you done?'

'I bumped into that bloody stupid chair you always put there. Hit me right in the balls.' Just before he fell through the door, Kate said, 'Don't leave me too long. Come and tell me what's happening.'

The moment he had gone she swung out of bed and went into the bathroom. There was no way she was going to receive the police without a bit of salvage work on her face.

Downstairs, Tony ventured into the dining room and approached the french windows. Now there was no sign of the police and their torches. He heard the front doorbell ring and went to answer it, remembering to disarm the burglar alarm before donning an overcoat from the hatstand and switching on the porch lights. Satisfied that it was the police outside, he opened the door and was confronted by a disconcertingly young sergeant wearing an orange fluorescent jacket over his uniform.

'Mr Chivers?'

'Yes, thanks so much for responding so quickly.'

'Well, we've had a good look around, sir, but haven't found anything. You say you heard a scream?'

'Several, yes. Very close by, the last just under our bedroom window in fact. It sounded like a girl, definitely female.'

The sergeant looked straight at Tony. 'Or a vixen, perhaps, sir?'

'Sorry?'

'Vixen, sir. A fox. They come scavenging, 'specially this time of year when there's not much around.'

'You think it was a fox?' Tony said slowly.

'Judging from the footprints in the snow, sir, yes. He definitely wasn't wearing Reeboks unless they make them in size one.'

'Well, I never. A fox, eh?'

Three other uniformed policemen plus an Alsatian came up behind the sergeant. All of them seemed the same age.

185

'Nothing,' the dog-handler reported. 'She got a scent, but it led to the fence, and then she lost interest.'

Kate came downstairs wearing her best silk dressing gown. 'Everything all right, darling?'

'Yes, fine,' Tony replied weakly. 'The sergeant says it was a fox. Isn't that amazing? It sounded so human, didn't it?'

'They do, sir. Mistake anybody could make.'

Now Roger and Evelyn both appeared on the landing. 'Anything wrong, Tony?' Roger asked.

'No, nothing to worry about. Just a false alarm.'

'Sure?'

'Absolutely.' To conceal a growing feeling of foolishness he turned back to the policemen. 'Since we dragged you out on a cold night, would you like to come in for a coffee?'

'Well, that wouldn't come amiss, sir. Thank you very much.'

'I'll just put her back in the van,' the dog-handler said, as the other three trooped inside.

'Good evening . . . I mean good morning,' Kate said. 'How awful to make such a mistake. As my husband said, we were convinced somebody was being attacked.' She led the way into the kitchen and immediately put the kettle on. 'We've got some Christmas cake too, if you'd like it.'

'Or a turkey sandwich,' Tony put in helpfully. Kate grimaced at him.

'Just the coffee will be fine. Sure it's not putting you to too much trouble?'

'No, not at all. You're the ones who've had the trouble.'

Like Tony, Kate thought the policemen seemed incredibly young. 'Have you been on duty all night?'

'Since nine,' one of them replied. 'Until seven.'

Kate glanced at the kitchen clock: it showed half past one. She and Tony had only been in bed just over an hour. While she made the coffee, in his embarrassment Tony felt obliged to keep up a conversation. The policemen stood awkwardly, holding their flat caps.

'That looked a splendid dog,' Tony began. 'Not a foxhound, though,' with a weak attempt at humour.

'No,' the handler said with a blank face. 'She's a bitch.'

'Ah! D'you think dogs are a good deterrent?'

'Depends which breed, sir.'

'At the moment we've only got a killer cat. We had a Yorkie once, didn't we darling? Fred, quite a character. Barked a lot, but that was about all, mostly at anybody in uniform.' He was grateful for their weak smiles. 'Went for me once when I forgot my keys and tried to crawl in through the window. That was his crowning achievement. If one got a guard dog, what would you recommend?'

'German shepherd, Doberman. Got to be a good one, properly trained. Some of them can turn. Bitches are best. A bad dog is trouble.'

'I imagine. What's your opinion of burglar alarms?'

'A blessed nuisance, sir, from our point of view,' the sergeant replied. He blew on his coffee.

'And not much good,' one of his colleagues added.

'Really?'

'Well, sir, they probably put off the amateurs, but your professional thief isn't bothered. No, he'll know exactly what he's come for, get in, take it and scarper before we've had time to answer.'

'That's comforting, isn't it, darling? The insurance insist we have it.'

'Ah, well, yes, gives them an out, doesn't it, if you forget to turn it on. Read the fine print.'

Tony switched subjects. 'Has it been a quiet Christmas for you so far?'

'Average,' the sergeant said. 'Two bad car accidents and a knifing, woman took against her husband. Knifings are usually domestic.'

'Hear that, darling?'

'Yes, you'd better watch it,' Kate said.

'I can't get over it,' Tony offered round the slices of cake, 'thinking that was a girl and all the time it was a fox. It was such an awful cry . . . We know we've got badgers, but they don't make a noise, do they?'

'That was very welcome,' the sergeant said, putting down his empty cup. 'Went down a treat.' He and his colleagues edged for the door. 'Well, glad it was nothing serious.'

'We really feel stupid,' Kate said, 'calling you out.'

'That's what we're here for, madam.'

'Wait a minute,' Tony said. He disappeared, coming back a few minutes later with four paperback copies of one of his novels. 'Hope you haven't read my latest. These wouldn't be considered bribery, would they? Let me sign them for you, or would you prefer them unsigned as being rarer?'

'That's very nice of you, sir,' the sergeant said. 'Could you sign it to the wife? She's the reader.'

'Pleasure. What's her name?'

'Beatrice . . . Put Beattie.'

Tony did the honours for all four.

'Appreciate that, sir. Well, good-night Mrs Chivers and thank you again for the coffee.'

Tony saw them out. 'What a berk thing to do.'

'Darling, it could have been something. I thought the same thing. Weren't they sweet? Two of them looked like teenagers.'

'Well, another drama over,' Tony said. 'I notice Martin slept through it.' He munched on a piece of cake. 'Mention of old Fred made me think maybe we should get another dog.'

'No, thank you. He finished me for dogs.'

'You loved Fred.'

'He was a nightmare. All our animals turn into nightmares because you spoil them.'

'Fred had some endearing qualities, though.'

'Like farting.'

'Only when he was old.'

'We're going to be old in the morning if we don't get to bed. I was in the middle of such a wonderful sleep.'

Tony programmed the alarm again and they started up the stairs. 'Did you know Martin and Evelyn are leaving tomorrow?' she said as they climbed into bed. 'You're not going to read, are you?'

'Just for a moment, to get myself calm again.'

'I can't sleep with the light on.'

'Okay.' He put the book down and switched off his bedside lamp. They lay in the darkness without speaking for a while, then Kate said: 'Patricia's the one I feel sorry for. Martin just drifts through everything. He drifted through school and now he's drifting through university. He's twenty for God's sake, about time he grew up.'

'Well, there's nothing like getting a girl pregnant to make you grow up quickly.'

'Did you ever? Before me?'

He thought carefully before answering, not wishing to lie outright. 'I had a similar scare once.'

There was an appreciable pause before Kate said: 'What d'you think we should do? You're so good about these things. What if she decides to have the baby? They're both so young.'

'Being young and having children isn't necessarily a bad thing.' He knew, with chill certainty, that although she had passed over his last reply there would be a moment in the future when she would return to the subject.

'But what will they live on? Where would they get the money?'

'You're lying next to it, I expect,' he said lightly – many a truth being said in jest during the hours of darkness. 'Let's cross that bridge when we come to it. I thought you wanted to get to sleep.'

'I want a new head, that's what I want.' She turned over, putting a gap between them, always a sign that his answer had been the wrong one.

Fifteen

There were footprints in the snow, two sets, criss-crossing each other – the fox's and the larger impressions of the police tracker dog. Tony had felt compelled to look for himself the moment he got up, going into the garden wearing his dressing gown and gum boots. Emily joined him, bounding forward a few feet at a time in the deep snow, as though on a switchback. She rubbed against his legs.

'Come on in, you,' Tony said. He stroked the stiff fur, then squelched his way back to the kitchen, pulling the gum boots free on the doorstep. It was only then that he saw what time it was – gone ten o'clock. They'd overslept, not surprising really, given the events of the night. 'Lucky the fox didn't get you,' he said to the cat as he put its food down. He lit a cigarette, needing a jolt of nicotine to get himself into operating mode, before measuring out the coffee beans. As he reached for the grinder he found a note stuck to it with Sellotape.

'Dear Mummy and Dad, you were still asleep so we didn't disturb you. Evelyn and I wanted to get off early in case the roads were bad. Will ring when I get there. Thanks for a great Xmas. Don't worry. Love Martin. P.S. Evelyn says thank you too, she's left a letter for Mummy on the hall table.'

While he waited for the coffee to percolate Tony did what he often did first thing in the morning: went to his computer. He switched on and waited for the first menu to come up on the screen, then keyed in to his word-processing software. Another key stroke and the text appeared. He stared at it, corrected a couple of spelling mistakes, then deleted the last paragraph before wandering back to the kitchen to see if the coffee was ready. He hated what he had just read.

He found Roger, dressed, and helping himself to some breakfast. 'Found everything you want?'

'Yes, thanks. What happened during the night?'

'You didn't hear anything?'

'No. What should I have heard?'

'It was the darnedest thing,' Tony said. 'I could have sworn I heard a girl screaming. Woke me up and I called the police. Turned out to be a vixen. Did I look stupid. They were very nice about it.'

'Well, always better to be safe than sorry. Look, I've already outstayed my welcome, so I'm pushing off today.'

'You don't have to.'

'I must,' Roger said, 'for more reasons than one. As a matter of fact I've got an interview for a new job this morning. At least I'll be sober for it,' he added with a touch of humour that had long been absent. 'But since we've broken the ice, I'll be in touch.'

'We have a lunch date, remember? You just tell me when.'

'Is Kate up?'

'Not yet, I was just going to take her a cup of coffee.'

'Well, say goodbye for me . . . And thank you both.'

'Keep in touch with Pop, too, if you can. It means a lot to him.'

'Yes, I know. I will as soon as I get things straightened out.'

'Good luck with the job,' Tony said.

Taking the coffee up to Kate he found she was still asleep. He waited for a few seconds at the foot of the bed in case her eyes opened, thinking how good she looked in the mornings, unlike himself. Her skin had a faintly olive bloom which made him believe that somewhere in the past her family had come from Italy. He left her undisturbed and returned to his study to pick up the threads.

*

At that same moment Martin was kissing Evelyn goodbye. They were standing in the hallway of her small, semi-detached house, in the industrial quarter of Oxford, a legacy of her divorce. The house was cold from being left over the holiday period, and there was a certain mustiness about it. The Laura Ashley print wallpaper stamped it in the eighties, and the framed Bernard Buffet lithographs lining the staircase added to the impression that, although Evelyn might have moved on, her surroundings had remained in a time-warp.

Feeling that the occasion demanded it, he kissed her full on the lips, but escape was uppermost in his mind. She clung to him for the duration of the kiss then, as if reading his thoughts, gently pushed him away.

'You get off,' she said. 'Let me know how it goes.'

'Yes, I will.'

'I hope it all works out for the best.' I don't mean that, she thought, photographing his face for the times when he would not be there.

'I'll ring you later,' he said, edging towards the front door.

'Well, if you can.'

'Oh, I promise.'

He went to her again, this time kissing the side of her mouth. 'Thanks for being so understanding.'

Just go, she thought, before I cry. There were two Christmas cards still on the mat and she picked them up before opening the door for him. Again he hesitated before making the move.'Roads weren't too bad.'

'No, but be careful. Wear your belt.'

As she stood in the doorway and watched him drive away, she wished they had invented a device to protect the heart from the whiplash of a parting. She knew he would have pushed her to the back of his mind by the time he reached the main road. She picked up her overnight case and went upstairs to a bedroom and a bed that nobody shared.

Martin, for his part, drove away with a new-found lightness of spirit, relieved that the parting from Evelyn had been accomplished without a heavy scene. It's the right decision, he said to himself, whatever the outcome with Patricia, you didn't want to get involved there. He made himself believe that Patricia's revelation had provided the shock he needed; without it, he might have drifted on into a relationship he would have regretted.

He put the radio on. A girl was singing an old Gershwin number which, although not really appropriate for the occasion, was sentimental enough to suit his mood. He hummed along with her until she was faded out for a commercial, momentarily losing concentration and nearly driving through a red light.

Having had her fill of sharing digs, Deborah,

Patricia's friend, lived on the other side of town in what estate agents euphemistically termed 'a studio apartment', evoking a false picture of an artist's romantic garret. In Deborah's case the reality was a cheap conversion of a second-storey room in an Edwardian house, measuring maybe eighteen by twenty feet, which provided some living space, a small kitchen, an even smaller bathroom and a bedroom on a shelf reached by a ladder. Far from having a studio's north light, the only window faced east onto the back wall of a supermarket. 'Not the greatest view,' Deborah was fond of explaining, 'but at least I don't have to go far to shop. And you get a preview of all the latest graffiti.'

She was totally different from Patricia both in temperament and appearance, inclined to be over-weight whereas Patricia was slim. Her hair was a vivid russet colour which a lot of people suspected came out of a bottle but was in fact genuine, and she insisted on wearing clothes that drew attention to her weak points. Some of their friends had unkindly nicknamed them Laurel and Hardy, which was un-fair to both. It was undoubtedly true that Patricia was the more outwardly attractive of the two, but Deborah had qualities which, although not so obvi-ous on first meeting, grew on acquaintance – namely a great sense of humour and a willingness to put herself out for friends. Her weight might have both-ered others, but left her indifferent. She liked eating, and the constant frenzy about diet and exercise in magazines and the media bored her. 'I do take exercise,' she said when asked the question, 'I climb that ladder to bed every night.' Her love of junk food would have turned many of the pilgrims looking backwards on the road to anorexia into blocks of salt.

Patricia, on the other hand, belonged to that irritating band who could eat anything without it making the slightest difference and this, as much as anything else, gave a curious twist to a friendship devoid of bickering about each other's faults. Because they were such opposites they had never engaged in the war of the sexes: there was no rivalry over boyfriends, so often the cause of rifts between some in their circle. Patricia might give the impression to strangers of being an ice maiden, but Martin had cause to know otherwise. More the earth mother type, Deborah could be laughed into bed and such is the selection of the species, tended to favour small men who were drawn to her like flies to sticky paper, confident that, whatever else, they would not be bored in her company. Neither was promiscuous; they listened to the warnings about the HIV virus that had cast such a blight over their generation, but at the same time the dictates of their bodies were not to be denied. They and their friends had a fatalistic attitude that perhaps had only been imitated once before when another generation of the same age had, beyond all reason, accepted the horrors of the Somme.

No such sombre considerations were uppermost in Martin's mind as he neared his destination; he could not wait for the reunion, convincing himself that his destiny had been decided for him. Perhaps it would be the making of him, he would confound his parents by suddenly becoming the responsible son they had always wanted. He would dry Patricia's tears, convince her that the brief excursion with Evelyn was nothing more than a passing peccadillo, a mild sowing of wild oats that had served to strengthen his love for her. He had a vision of them together, a vision not unconnected to the lyrics of the pop songs they both enjoyed, since those provided the parameters of their shared emotions. He would get a part-time job, study hard to obtain his degree, drop in rather than out as everybody expected him to. The only distant blot on the future landscape was Patricia's parents, but for the moment he dismissed their reaction rather in the way that a complacent general, far from the front lines, ignores the strength of the enemy in his preparations for battle.

There was a profound sense of anticlimax when he finally arrived and climbed the steep stairs to Deborah's flat, only to find that Patricia wasn't there and to be greeted with: 'Hello, you shit.'

'Don't start off like that.'

199

'I always start as I mean to finish.' She smiled as she said it, but Martin remained wary.

'But Pat is coming, isn't she?' he panted.

'Sure, but she said it was touch and go with the holy parents,' Deborah said. 'She had to lie like crazy and pretend I desperately needed her help with my thesis. They'd arranged for her to go with them to a performance of the *Messiah*.'

Barefooted and wearing only a cotton kimono, she fussed around picking up scattered magazines and clothes. 'You look frozen. Want a coffee or some of this punch I made yesterday?'

Her flat seemed smaller than ever, and he eased himself around a Christmas tree that took up a quarter of the space and settled himself into one of the two armchairs to huddle close to her electric fire.

'Did she say when she might get here?'

'Well, I was expecting her before now. Don't worry. She's desperate to see you for obvious reasons. You both want your heads examined.'

'Well, I didn't run from it, did I? I'm here. How did she sound?'

'Like she was climbing the wall.'

'I haven't exactly been enjoying life since she told me.'

'Tough titty, my heart bleeds for you.' Deborah poured the punch into two mugs decorated with sayings she had written with a marker pen. Martin's read: 'One Kafka is enough.'

'Did you have a good Christmas?' he said, taking a first sip. It tasted of boiled face-cloths laced with cinnamon and U-boat fuel, but he managed to swallow it without gagging.

'Not bad. I had a party here and I made about three gallons. What d'you think?'

'Interesting. You should patent it.'

'I'll give you the recipe if you like.'

'Give it to the IRA, they could use it instead of Semtex. By the way, you know my sister's married to an officer out there? He was blown up by that bomb on Christmas Day.'

'Really? God how awful.'

'He wasn't killed, just injured. But you can imagine, what with that, my drama and my grandfather having to go into hospital, it's been a rough three days ... Why're you laughing?'

'Sorry, I didn't mean to. But you have to admit your Christmas sounds like a disaster movie.' The atmosphere thawed slightly as she changed the subject. 'Tell you something I'm into now – salsa. You know that enormous American, Terry, who's taking Classics at Magdalen?'

'Don't think so.'

'Yes, you do. He goes with that little *Madame Butterfly* freak, she of the monster eyelashes, very submissive, like they bound her brain at birth? He's from Texas, you must remember him – looks like one of the Harlem Globetrotters.'

'Oh him, yes. Met him once.'

'I told everybody "bring a bottle" on the invite, and he turns up with this enormous jar of the stuff.'

'What is salsa?'

'Try some.' She produced the jar from the kitchen and spread a dollop on a piece of Ryvita. 'Here, I'm just crazy about it, been eating it all day. You know me, never do anything by halves.' Too late she added, 'You might find it a bit hot,' as Martin dutifully took a mouthful and immediately choked.

'Christ! What's it got in it?'

'Chillies and spanish fly. Just kidding. Personally I like spicy things. Take some more punch with it.'

'No thanks, they might ignite each other. Was it a good party?'

'I guess so. First Christmas in ages I haven't gone home, because, all joking apart, I do have to finish my pissy thesis. D'you like these?' She rummaged behind her chair and held up a bra and bikini panties. 'Present to myself. Sent off for them from a catalogue. Victoria's Secret they're called.'

'They look like an open secret,' Martin said.

'Want me to put them on for a gag?'

'God no!' he said genuinely alarmed. 'Pat'll be here soon. Look you know her better than anybody . . . how d'you think she'll be?'

'Bloody scared.'

'Apart from that?'

'What d'you think? You acted like a shit.'

'It wasn't entirely me. She was the one who ended it all.'

'You behaved like a real prick, admit it. Going off with Whistler's mother.'

'Evelyn's not that old. Anyway there was nothing in it. I was upset and she just happened to be around.'

'Yeah, like the spider woman.'

'No, crap. She was just being kind.'

'Gave you a padded bra to cry on, did she?'

'Ha ha.' Martin jumped as the Entryphone sounded. He swung round and from where he sat he could see a distorted image of Patricia on the minute screen. Deborah pushed the door-release button and a few moments later he heard Patricia coming up the stairs.

'Just be nice to her,' Deborah warned.

'Of course I will.' He stood up as Patricia came in. In his ignorance, Martin had been half expecting her condition to be visible, but she was muffled up in an assortment of sweaters which rendered her shapeless. She didn't look at him straight away, but concentrated on Deborah.

'Sorry I'm late, Debbo, but they argued right up to the last minute. In the end I just stormed out and left them to it.'

She started to take two of the sweaters off and it was only after she had thrown them down that she turned to Martin.

'Hello.'

'Hi. Glad you could make it. Here, have this chair.'

'Listen you two,' Deborah said, climbing up to the shelf where she had her bed, 'I know you'll miss me, but I'm going to leave you alone while I go out and get some grub.' She grabbed some clothes off the bed and descended again. 'What does anybody fancy? Kentucky Fried or a Big Mac?'

'Nothing for me,' Patricia said.

'Martin?'

'I'll have a Big Mac. D'you want any money?'

'Pay me when I get back,' Deborah replied as she went into the bathroom to change.

'Aren't you hungry?' Martin asked.

'Not very.'

'How d'you feel otherwise?'

'So-so.'

'Is it okay to smoke?'

'If you want.'

'Won't make you sick or anything, will it?'

'Don't suppose so, my father smokes all the time.'

'You haven't told them anything, have you?'

'God, no.'

Deborah emerged from the bathroom and put on her topcoat. 'Shan't be too long,' she said and left.

'How does she sleep up there?' Martin said. 'Must be claustrophobic.'

'She's used to it.'

'I haven't slept much since you told me.' He still didn't know whether to touch her. 'Don't suppose you have either. I'm really sorry it happened. I thought we'd been careful.'

'So did I,' Patricia said, and he realised with relief that she wasn't going to cry.

'You're pretty sure, are you? I mean, you've checked the dates and everything? Well, course you must have . . . Listen, about Evelyn . . . I know that upset you, but I was upset too because you wouldn't hear me out.'

'Did she go home with you for Christmas?'

'Yes.'

'That must have been nice.'

'Look, don't let's start again. It's finished. I'm not going to see her again unless I bump into her at college. Debbie's right, I was really shitty, don't think I don't know it.'

'Did you go to bed with her?'

'No!'

'I won't mind if you tell me now, I just don't want to find out later.'

'Promise I didn't.'

'Did she ask you to?'

'No.'

'I bet she thought about it. Especially when you invited her home. What did your parents think of her? They must have been surprised.'

'Yeah, they were. They seemed to get on all right,

well they would, she's more their age group. Pat, let's not go on about her, I want to talk about you, you and me. See, I've been thinking a lot ever since you phoned, and I don't want you to worry . . . My father gave me very good advice . . . '

Patricia stopped him. 'Does he know? Why did you tell him?'

'I had to. Nobody else I could tell.'

'Why did you tell anybody?'

'You told Deborah.'

'That's different.'

'Well, okay, but . . . if anything had to be done, not that we're going to do anything, I'm not saying we have to or will, I'd have to go to him for the . . . you know, money. That's all,' he ended lamely.

'You've made plans for that already, have you? Is that what you talked about to your father?'

'No. That came into it. Not from me. He brought it up.'

'And what did you say?'

'Nothing.'

'You must have said something.'

'I didn't, I just listened.'

'I bet he said she must have an abortion.'

'Cross my heart he didn't.'

'Well, I'm not, no matter what anybody says and you may as well know that right away.'

'I agree. If you'd only let me say something.'

'Go on then.'

He paced the small room, circumventing the furniture, giving himself time to think of the right words. 'What I've been thinking . . . what I've decided . . . and I didn't know what you'd feel like, did I? . . . If you could forget I behaved like a shit . . . and you still felt the same way about me, if things went back to where they were before, and you wanted the baby, I'd somehow face your parents and say we wanted to get married. That's what I thought . . . '

He stopped and waited. Patricia sat staring at the bar of the electric fire.

'My father would probably kill you if he ever found out the truth,' she said finally.

'Well, that would put the kibosh on it, wouldn't it? I couldn't marry you if I was dead.'

The pathetic joke broke the tension between them at long last and they both laughed, the laughter becoming tears in Patricia's case, and Martin went and knelt by the side of her chair. They clung to each other exchanging terms of endearment, using those trite, coded phrases that all lovers invent for themselves and which have no meaning for others.

'You're not just saying all that to make me feel better, are you?' Patricia asked as he dried her eyes with a handkerchief that was none too clean.

'I mean it.'

Their kisses became more prolonged and passionate and before long he had his hand inside her sweater and was fondling her breasts. The release they both felt propelled them onto a roller-coaster that could not be stopped. Soon they were semi-naked, Martin using familiar skills to arouse her. 'Let's use Debbie's bed, we can't do it here,' he whispered against her groin. She put up no resistance as he led her by the hand and they both climbed to the shelf, tumbling onto the unmade bed as the last of their clothes were kicked off. Martin gently touched her stomach.

'It can't harm the baby, can it?'

'Don't be silly,' she answered. 'I looked it up in a book. You can do it until six or seven months.'

He had a sudden thought. 'I haven't got anything with me.'

'Doesn't matter now, does it? Quickly, put it in, I want you so badly, I can't wait, do me . . . ' She became incoherent as he willingly obliged, losing himself in an all-consuming act that twenty-four hours previously he had believed he would never experience again.

Happily dazed they didn't hear Deborah return until a voice from below said, 'Oh, charming. I assume you've kissed and made up or were you just making the bed for me?'

They slid to the end of the bed and peered down through the shelf-rail, happily guilty.

'It's all right, we're going to get married,' Patricia said.

It was only then, his arm resting on her warm shoulders, that Martin fully realised that he had taken the first step down an unknown road.

Sixteen

'We've got enough uneaten food for a remake of *Caligula*,' Kate said, surveying the contents of her refrigerator the following morning. 'Just look at it. I suppose I could make some turkey hamburgers and freeze them. D'you fancy those tonight?'

She turned around but Tony had left the kitchen and she shouted after him: 'What d'you want for dinner? Can you face turkey again if I jazz it up?'

'No, thanks.'

'Well, what then?'

'I'm easy. How about bacon and eggs, something simple?' he shouted back.

It was so typical of a man, she thought. Nothing's simple in a bloody kitchen. I want to be liberated, burn my bra and *flamber* the sodding turkey over it, give him that for dinner. She longed for the promised holiday to materialise, for somebody else to prepare a meal and just put it in front of her for once. '*I'm easy,*' she said, parodying Tony's response. She pushed some soggy trifle down the waste disposal, then switched on the radio for company, hoping to find a music programme, but it was a heated discussion on whether women should be ordained, conducted with a marked lack of Christian charity between a bishop (anti), who sounded as if he was ready for the sex change, and a woman (pro), who had already had it. 'Oh, do me a favour, who cares?' Kate said, turning them off.

She sniffed at a bowl of cream, decided it was sour and binned it, together with a plate of cocktail sausages, a half-eaten tub of yoghurt and a tired lettuce. She was just about to junk the jar of pickled cucumbers but gave it a stay of execution when she remembered that Pop would be returning. Contemplating what still remained, she felt defeated by it all. Although it was only eleven o'clock she did something out of character and poured herself a glass of white wine. Maybe I'll get drunk, she thought, why not? But the wine tasted bitter in her mouth and she poured it down the sink.

Hearing the cat flap squeak, she turned ready to vent her frustrations on the animal and suddenly screamed.

'Oh, my God! Tony! Tony! come quickly!'

'What? What is it? What have you done?'

'Just come here!'

He rushed into the kitchen. 'Have you burnt yourself?'

'No, look what that hideous cat of yours has just brought in.'

Lying just inside the back door was the stiffened corpse of a rabbit.

'Get it out, get it out,' Kate urged. 'Wait, don't pick it up with your hands. Put these gloves on. Urgh, it's revolting.'

'Don't panic, don't panic, I'll deal with it.'

'That animal is turning into a serial killer.'

'It's their nature to kill things, you can't change that.'

'Well, it's a very nasty nature.'

Putting on the kitchen gloves, Tony bent and picked up the rabbit with outstretched arms.

'It's probably covered in maggots.'

'Open the door for me . . . no, wait.' He peered more closely at the corpse. 'You know what this is, don't you?'

'Course I know what it is, it's a dead rabbit.'

'It's *their* rabbit.'

'Whose?'

'Next door's. The Harrisons. It's their beady little girl's bloody pet rabbit.'

'How can you tell?'

'I can tell because I've seen her playing with it in the garden. Look, it's got a collar on. She dotes on this rabbit.'

'Well, she won't be doting any longer.'

'They're sure to blame Emily. They're always

complaining she scratches up the flower beds and goes to sleep on their fucking begonias. Remember how they insisted she was the one who frightened all the budgies to death in their aviary.'

'Well, it probably was, that cat's capable of anything. Why you ever called her Emily is beyond me. She should have been named Lucretia.'

'I didn't choose Emily, that was Jenny. Don't sidetrack me. Harrison's got a very nasty disposition. I know him, he could turn really ugly over this. Only one thing for it.'

'What?'

'We've got to put it back.'

Kate stared at him. 'Have you gone mad? Put it back where?'

'In the hutch. Listen to me. They've gone away. I know that because I saw him in the village and the smug bastard was boasting how they always spend Christmas in a hotel. If we smarten it up and get it back in the hutch before they come home, they won't be any the wiser.'

'You are mad.' She watched in amazement as he took the corpse to the sink. 'What're you doing now?'

'I'm going to wash it.' He turned on the hot tap. 'Can't put it back like this, it's all covered in earth.'

'I don't believe you're doing this,' she said as he squeezed some liquid soap and started to shampoo the rabbit.

'You watch, it'll come up like new,' he said,

warming to the task. 'Can you get me some conditioner? And I'll need your hair-dryer.'

'You're not having my dryer.'

'Don't get manic, it won't damage it. When I've washed it, I'll blow-dry it, fluff up the fur, otherwise it won't look right. Look, see? It's a hundred per cent better already.'

'I think you've gone insane.'

'You wait until you see the finished result. I'll put it in the garage and then climb over their fence when it's dark. Don't look so worried.' He lifted the sodden rabbit out of the sink and smelt it. 'It pongs a bit. We might have to spray it with perfume.'

'We are not going to spray it with anything,' Kate said. 'Why don't you take it to the beauty parlour and have its nails manicured while you're at it? I'm amazed you haven't thought of mouth-to-mouth resuscitation. I really do believe you've flipped. What if you're caught?'

'I won't be caught. There! That's a big improvement. Fetch me the hair-dryer. If a job's worth doing it's worth doing properly.'

'Tony, you need to see somebody, get psychiatric help.'

'All right, you come up with a better idea. I'm telling you if this thing is missing when boring little Goldilocks comes home, all hell will break loose. Harrison will have a cardiac arrest. He's the sort of man who might take us to court.'

'Even Harrison is hardly likely to take a cat to court.'

'We're the owners, they'll get at Emily through us.'

'But even if you do put it back, it'll still be dead.'

'Well it'll look as if it died of natural causes.'

'After having a perm.'

'You can joke, but it'll look great by the time I'm done. You see.'

Reluctantly, she went upstairs and fetched the dryer. 'You can throw those gloves away when you've finished,' she said when she returned. 'I'm not putting them on again. Here.' She handed him the dryer. Tony laid the limp corpse on some kitchen paper and began the final restoration.

'This is out of a horror movie,' Kate said as she watched. 'Imagine if this got into the papers. "Ghoulish practices of well-known novelist. Tony Chivers committed." '

'Where's your spirit of adventure? Look it's fluffing up like new. I thought this would do the trick. It's got quite a sweet expression now. Look.'

'Don't bring it near me. Get out, you!' she said to Emily who was staring at the proceedings with an expectant look on her face. 'I'm going to leave you to it, I don't want to be part of it.'

Left to himself Tony applied the dryer until he was satisfied, then sprayed the rabbit with Summer Breeze air freshener, stepping back to admire his handiwork. The animal now had some semblance of life – enough, he thought, to fool the Harrisons at first glance when next they looked into the hutch. Satisfied at last, he carried the rabbit into the garage and after some thought placed it on the back seat of the Volvo. It took him a while to prod the dead animal into a feasible pose. He closed the car door, walked away, then went back and took a quick look: yes, anybody seeing it for the first time would definitely be taken in.

He felt curiously elated.

That night after a further argument with Kate he put on a black track suit and prepared for the final part of the operation.

'Shouldn't you wear white?' Kate said from the bed. 'You'll be seen for miles going out like that in the snow.'

'I don't happen to have a white track suit.'

'Put a sheet over your head then. If you're caught you can pretend you're playing Trick or Treat out of season.'

'Oh, it's easy to sit there and criticise. I'm the one who has to do it.' He pulled a Balaclava over his head and put on gloves.

'I'm not forcing you. How d'you know they haven't come back already?'

'Because there are no lights. I checked.'

He went to the window and peered out. 'Seems quiet.'

'Shouldn't we synchronise watches, isn't that what they do?'

'Oh, very funny.'

'What about footprints? You'll leave footprints behind.'

'I've thought of that, believe it or not. I shall cover my tracks on the return journey. I don't think I've forgotten anything.'

'Only your brain.'

'Aren't you going to wish me luck?'

'No. I'll try and think up an alibi while you're gone.'

He scowled and left the room. After getting a plastic bag, small brush and torch, he went through into the garage. The rabbit had slumped a little, but he felt it still looked presentable. Putting everything in the bag, he opened the garage doors cautiously, then set off.

He had no sooner gone a few yards when he was joined by an interested Emily. 'Piss off,' he said, 'I don't want you with me, it's your neck I'm trying to save. Shoo!'

Keeping close to his own boundary until he reached the fence between the two properties and making sure that there was still no sign that the Harrisons were back, he dropped the bag with the rabbit over the fence, then cocked one leg onto the top rail. The fence quivered ominously but took his weight. Once over he retrieved the bag and started towards the hutch, but after a few yards he stopped.

'Fuck!' he hissed, 'I know what I've forgotten. Damn!'

Leaving the rabbit behind, he retraced his steps, climbed back over the fence and went back inside the house. Kate was in the kitchen making herself a cup of tea.

'That was quick.'

'I haven't done it yet. I want a carrot.' He went to the fridge and rummaged in the vegetable drawer. He selected a carrot and then proceeded to nibble tiny bites out of it.

'How does that look?' he asked, holding it up for Kate's inspection.

'You worried about night-blindness?'

'It's not for me. I'm going to stuff this in the rabbit's mouth as a final touch.'

'Perfection. He died having the last supper.'

'Are you being sarcastic again?'

'As if I would.'

He left her and repeated his previous manoeuvre. Not wishing to use the torch in the open he had some anxious moments locating the hutch and was sweating profusely by the time he found it. Lifting the rabbit from the bag carefully so as not to disarrange it, he reached in. The stench of old rabbit pee, like undiluted ammonia, made him reel back, but he managed to hold his breath long enough to wedge the rabbit upright with the aid of its water bowl. Only then did he switch on the torch to apply the final

218

touches. His master-stroke of the carrot didn't come off because he could not force the mouth open to take it. Instead he placed it between the animal's stiff paws. One final look, and he closed the hutch door and slid the bolt home.

The journey back to the fence took much longer since he had to pause at every step and brush his footprints smooth. By the time he was safely back inside his own kitchen the track suit was wringing wet.

'Here,' Kate greeted him with a large whisky. 'I'm sure you need this, Raffles. Look at you, you're soaked.'

'Mission accomplished,' he said. 'All our aircraft returned safely. Now say I'm an idiot.'

'You're an idiot.'

Seventeen

Unaware of her father's wanderings the night before, Jenny sat in her Belfast hotel room contemplating the sea of plastic that constitutes the state-of-the-art breakfasts now standard throughout the civilised world. Always conscious of her health she had ordered half a grapefruit, toast and coffee – a simple enough request. The order arrived with white bread, which appeared to have been previously used as a shower mat, half a grapefruit, requiring a Black & Decker power-drill to penetrate it, and all the other ingredients sealed in containers that would have baffled the bomb disposal squad: the packaged long-life milk, and the portions of butter and marmalade seemed to have been designed for a race of midgets with sharp fingernails, fascinated by puzzles. There was a personal message from the management on the tray, together with a single carnation, both presumably intended to give an air of festivity to the proceedings.

Rain oozed down from a grey sky outside her window and the country of the travel brochures seemed far away, a Xanadu conjured by pixie imaginations to entice the unwary. She knew she was being unfair, but she was frightened; the slightest external noise – a car backfiring, the wail of an ambulance – gave her palpitations, for she felt that, as an Army officer's wife, she was a potential target. It was no good her telling herself she was being irrational and stupid, the feeling would not go away. It wasn't that everybody she had met hadn't been kindness itself, and although she found the nasal accent difficult to understand, there was no mistaking the stoic friendliness. The hospital staff in particular had gone out of their way to comfort her and she knew that Andy was getting the best medical attention. It was just that she had never been in a war zone before and, despite the fact that the majority of the local inhabitants had conditioned themselves over the years to regard the Troubles as something to be ignored, she could not rid herself of Bosnia-like comparisons. It was the feeling of being a total stranger, isolated with no known signposts to guide her.

She pushed the breakfast tray aside – by now piled with debris, none of it environmentally friendly – and dragged herself to the bathroom. There were warning notices on the backs of the doors, giving explicit instructions in the event of an emergency, a further reminder to somebody like herself of the dangers that lurked. She showered, afterwards carefully applying her make-up so as to look her best when next she visited Andy, hoping that Elizabeth Arden would help mask her fears from him. When dressed she sat on the edge of the bed leafing through a fashion magazine, the pictures in which bore no resemblance to everyday life, but were the product of an enclosed little world peopled by the ultra-rich who apparently clothed themselves in creations that could only be worn for Mardi Gras. The images – the bored perfection of the models' faces and bodies, frozen in poses that accentuated the idiocy of what they were displaying – seemed to have sprung from people who had never walked ordinary streets. What seemed to Jenny particularly obscene was that one layout had the mega-models posturing in an African shanty town alongside wide-eyed, naked children. She put the magazine aside and glanced at the digital bedside clock-radio to see how long before her escort arrived to take her to the hospital.

On an impulse she picked up the phone and dialled home, but before anybody answered she suddenly felt a wave of nausea. Hanging up, she rushed to the bathroom and was violently sick. That's all I need, she thought, to be taken ill while I'm here, but the spasms gradually subsided and as she brushed her teeth a second time she put it down to the acid sourness of the grapefruit. Recovered, she dialled again and this time her father answered.

'Did you ring about ten minutes ago?' he asked.

'Yes, but it was a bad connection,' Jenny answered, not wishing to worry him with the real reason.

'So how is everything?'

'Well, Andy was much better when I left him last night. There's even a chance they may discharge him by the end of the week.'

'That's great . . . Kate! Darling, pick up your phone, it's Jenny . . . Tell your mother that.'

Kate came on the line. 'Darling. Is the news better?'

'Much better. I was just telling Daddy, Andy could be out of hospital by Saturday.'

'And then what? Will they let him come home?'

'Oh, yes, they'll fly us both home. I wanted to ask you about Pop. How is he?'

'Not too bad. We've got a family of invalids, haven't we? But how are you, darling, bearing up?'

'Yes, I'm fine. Missing not being home.'

'What's the hotel like?'

'Good, nothing special, they all look alike, don't they?'

'I've got a funny story to tell you when you get back.'

'Oh, tell me now, I need something funny.'

'Better not,' Tony interrupted. 'Never know who might be listening.'

'Like that, is it? Can't wait. Sounds intriguing.'

'No, I wouldn't say it was intriguing. I'll give you a blow by blow when we see you.'

'Darling, next time reverse the charges, don't run up bills. Will you be seeing Andy this morning?'

'Yes, I go in twice a day, Mummy.'

'Well, be sure and give him our love. I think about him all the time, poor boy.'

'Hardly a boy, Mummy.'

'Well, you know what I mean. Is it snowing there?'

'Sleet more than snow. Bloody cold though.'

'Wrap up warm when you go out.'

'Oh, Mummy, don't fuss so. I do take care of myself.' They chattered on for a few more minutes, exchanging those non-sequiturs that make up most family conversations, Kate unwilling to break the electronic umbilical cord. When, finally, they both hung up, she had tears in her eyes.

'I'm so glad they're both all right. I won't be happy until they're back here again,' she said to Tony.

'You are a moron, what're you crying for?'

'I'm not.'

'You heard her, she sounded great. Never need worry about Jenny, she's the tough one.'

'I know, I know, but I can't help it. Seeing those pictures on the news every night. And for what? None of them are ever going to change.'

'Hey!' Tony stopped her flow. 'Why don't we take a leaf out of the Harrisons' book and go out to lunch?'

'Where?'

'I'll find somewhere. How about Italian? Be a change, they don't do turkey pasta. Eh, how about it?'

'Yes, okay, that'll be lovely . . . Any sign of the Harrisons?'

'Not yet.'

'I keep thinking about what you did last night. You're crazy.'

'You're married to a genius, you realise that. I could have been a prominent taxidermist.'

Kate paused in the doorway. 'What about Pop?' she asked as an afterthought. 'We mustn't forget him.'

'We'll look in on the way back. Go on, go and fix your face and I'll make the booking.'

Twenty miles away, Martin had taken Deborah to lunch in the Little Chef where they both ordered the Special of the Day, basic sustenance that fitted Martin's pocketbook. He not only wanted to keep on the right side of her in his hour of need, he was also desperate for a confidante.

'D'you think any better of me now?' he asked.

'Time will tell . . . Yeah, you're only half a shit, I suppose.'

'Seriously, you do think we took the right decision?'

Deborah shrugged. 'I'm not really the one to ask. I mean, it isn't that I've got a hang-up about marriage, I just don't see the point of it. Have the baby by all means, but why not just live together? Why go through all that hassle?'

'You know why not. Pat says her old man would terminate me.'

'You ever been to a Catholic wedding?' Martin shook his head. 'I did once, over in Dublin, some cousin of my mother's got spliced. Now that's a *serious* Catholic country, not like here. I stayed in a bedroom that had a neon bleeding heart, can you believe? Illuminated blood running down the wall all night, drove me spastic. I mean, everywhere you looked J.C. and his mother were giving you a hard time. You want to miss that if you can. Because of course, they'll pressure you to become one.'

That jolted him afresh. 'Seriously?'

'Oh, sure.'

'But Pat doesn't believe any more than I do. She told me she's lapsed, if that's the right word, only goes to Mass when she's at home.'

'Yeah, but they think long-term. If they can't get you, they'll settle for the baby. Sign on the line, bonzo, swear to bring up this child according to the rules and regulations of Holy Rome. You wait. You're going to be knee-deep in priests.'

'Jesus . . . '

'And don't blaspheme, that earns you automatic penalty points.'

'I never thought of that. I guess you're right.'

'So, elope,' Deborah said. 'That's what I'd do.'

'Yeah, we talked about that, but there's my aged parents to think of as well as hers.'

'You told me your father was cool.'

'He is, he is . . . but I don't know about my mother,

226

she loves weddings, they're a big deal with her. She goes overboard on things like birthdays, Christmas.' He looked towards the counter. 'Would you like some pudding?'

'Why not?' She chose a vivid piece of cake, but Martin had suddenly lost his appetite, his thoughts clouded with images of the Spanish Inquisition transferred to Pinner. In turn these were replaced by more domestic horrors: Martin pushing a pram through the streets of Oxford, Martin attempting to study alongside a screaming baby. Love in the afternoon extracted long-term retribution it seemed.

When Deborah had demolished the technicolour cake, Martin paid the bill and they wandered outside.

'When're you supposed to face the music?'

'Tomorrow. Pat was going to prepare the way, you know, get them used to the idea that I might be thinking of something permanent, then I'm to go to tea tomorrow.'

'Teas are tricky. Why not dinner?'

'Because I'm not invited to dinner. Course I might be asked to stay on, depends how it goes.'

Somewhat bored with the subject, Deborah said: 'What d'you want to do now?'

'Go to a movie?'

'Yeah, that's a good idea. I tell you what I want to see, the new Woody Allen.'

'I heard that was depressing. One of his homages to Ingmar Bergman.'

227

'I like those. And if it's really deep it'll help me with my thesis. Yes?'

'Yes, if you want.' They walked to his car and he opened the passenger door for her. 'Tell you one other bit of family news. My uncle's become a Muslim. How about that?'

'Maybe that's the answer for you,' Deborah said, opening a tube of Smarties and beginning to chew. 'Go in and blast them with the Koran. Attack is the best means of defence.'

When Kate and Tony arrived at the hospital they were pleasantly surprised to find Pop fully dressed and sitting in a chair. His suitcase was on the bed.

'I told them you'd be here shortly,' was his greeting. 'Hoped you'd get here before the ambulance. They've given me my marching orders.'

'Well, thank goodness we got here in time. Would have been awful if you'd arrived and found we were out.'

Pop shook his head. 'No, I'm not going there, I'm going home.'

'Don't be silly, I wouldn't hear of it. You're to come back with us to be looked after.'

'No, I'd rather be in my own bed,' he said. 'I'm better off in my own place, with all my own things. Nothing wrong with me now. Look.' He pushed himself out of the chair and took a few steps. 'Right as rain.' He reached for the bed-rail.

Tony and Kate exchanged dubious glances.

'Not even for a few days? Until you're fully recovered.'

Pop shook his head. 'No, I tell you something Mother and I decided long ago. We both said whatever happened to us, we wouldn't be a burden. I'm all right. Got everything I want back there, and I know where everything is. Don't like change. I can do with it for a few days, then I like to get back to my own routine. They shave you here, you see. I like to shave myself.'

Kate thought, why should he be forced to do something he doesn't like? I wouldn't at his age. I don't like change either. She put her arms around him and hugged him. While in hospital he had lost the scent of tobacco she had always associated with him. Now his cheeks smelt of carbolic soap. 'Of course, Pop, if that's what you really want. But you're not going in an ambulance, we'll take you back, won't we Tony? Just let's drop by our house so I can pack you up some food. Shall we do that?'

'Up to you, love. Don't want to put you about.'

'Tony, go and tell them he doesn't need the ambulance. Now, Pop, have you got everything, nothing left in your bedside cupboard?'

'No, the nurse did it all.'

'Is this stick yours?'

'Yes, they gave me that.'

She handed the walking stick to him and offered an arm as they left the ward.

'What you could do for me is buy her some chocolates.'

'Who's that, Pop.'

'My nurse. Here, I've written her name down.' He paused and felt in his pocket.

'I asked her if she liked pickled cucumbers, but she's not like you, they don't agree with her. I think chocolates is best anyway.'

'I'm sure she'll be thrilled. I'll take care of it.'

He talked more about the nurse on the journey. It had been his first experience of hospital life and he spoke of it as though he personally had been administered to by a young Mother Teresa. Kate found his monologue infinitely touching; we must see him more often, she promised herself, it's awful that weeks go by and we don't make the effort. She was jolted from self-criticism as they turned the last corner into their street and she suddenly gripped Tony's thigh. He shot her an enquiring look.

'Did you see who we've just passed?' Kate said in a failed attempt to sound casual. 'The Harrisons are back.'

'They your neighbours, are they?'

'Yes, Pop.'

'I've got very good neighbours, I must say. On one side anyway. Look after me a treat. Don't know about chummy in number fifteen, though . . . can't quite place him. He's either a Turk or Canadian.'

'Really, Pop?' Kate was lost at that point,

picturing a lumberjack wearing a fez. 'That's nice for you.'

'What are yours like?'

'Well, we don't see much of them. They keep themselves to themselves.'

'Pity.'

Kate hurried inside as soon as Tony had parked. She disarmed the burglar alarm, then shouted on her way to the kitchen, 'You take care of Pop while I get the food for him.'

The two men went into the living room.

'Never liked doing that job,' the old man said.

'What's that, Pop?' Tony had moved nearer to the window and was looking across to the Harrisons' house.

'Taking down the tree. Your mother wouldn't do it, said it was my place.'

'No, they make a mess, don't they? Pine needles all over.' There was no sign of the Harrison child.

'How's the garden?' His father joined him at the window.

'Looking a bit sad at the moment.'

'They say snow's good for the ground.'

'Do they? I hope you're right.'

As he watched, the little Harrison girl suddenly appeared from out of the house.

'You can see right across there, can't you.'

'Yes. That was the storm. We lost all those trees.'

Even though it was at a distance and through glass,

Tony heard the child's scream. She came into view again, running back towards the house as Harrison came out to see what was wrong. Tony watched as the child gesticulated then flung herself into her father's arms to be comforted.

'When I had a garden, I wasn't too fond of trees. They keep the air from your rhubarb.'

'Do they? Yes,' Tony said, still distracted. 'That's a useful thing to know.'

'What're you both standing there for?' Kate said from the doorway.

'Pop was just looking at the state of the garden.'

'Well, he'll catch cold by the window. He's just come out of hospital. I'm ready if you are, Pop. I packed you enough for tonight and tomorrow, but you can always ring me if you want some more shopping done.'

As they went out into the hallway she pulled Tony back. 'Darling help me with the baskets.'

Knowing what she was going to ask the moment they were inside the kitchen, he whispered: 'They've found it.'

'Well, let's get out quickly.'

They rejoined the old man and got him into the car, this time taking the longer route so that they would not have to pass the Harrisons' house. Throughout the journey Kate tried desperately to think of some way she could ask Tony for more details, but inspiration failed her. It took them a good half an hour to get Pop settled in his own home and to light his fire. Tidying up the four-room flat on the ground floor of a block that looked as though the architect had majored in SS barracks, Kate had a renewed sense of guilt: all his possessions seemed so shabby, comfortless – the pattern of the carpet trod bare in places, the back of his armchair stained where his head rested, the crockery he used odd and chipped. The bathroom, in particular, dismayed her and she made a mental note to replace his tired bowl of shaving soap and buy him new towels. She mustn't overdo it, though; the sad familiarity obviously meant much to him, and you couldn't change people just because you found out more about them. Why did it take me this long? she thought, putting out a fresh pair of flannel pyjamas on his bed and slipping a hot water bottle between the sheets. It wasn't so difficult to understand why the nurse had made such an impression on him; it was the fact that a woman had cared for him after his years as a widower.

She carried these thoughts with her when they were back in the car and it wasn't until Tony said the word 'Harrison' that her own worries returned. 'He did what?' she said.

'The first thing that happened was the child came out, obviously found the rabbit stiff as a board and shouted for her father. Then Harrison appeared and he took a look.'

'Well, don't let's go back until later.'

'What difference will that make?'

'I don't know, I'm just terrified that he'll come knocking on the door.'

'There's nothing to connect us to it.'

'You sure?'

'Positive. I checked this morning and you couldn't see my footprints.'

'And you didn't leave your gloves or anything behind?'

'No. Stop worrying.'

'I can't help it. With our present luck I can't believe we'll get away with it. What would happen if he did somehow find out? Would you have to go to court? He could get you for trespassing, if nothing else.'

'Darling, all I did was to tart up a rabbit corpse. That's not a criminal offence. I could plead I did them a good turn, saved the child from having a more serious trauma.'

'Is that what you'd say?'

'No, I used that hypothetically.'

'Okay, if you really don't think there's anything to worry about.'

'Look at me. Do I look worried?'

'You wouldn't tell me if you were,' Kate said, having the last word.

Later that evening Kate was upstairs when she heard the front doorbell go. Looking out of the window she saw the lights of a police car in their drive. She hurried downstairs just in time to catch Tony as he came out of his study.

'It's the police,' she whispered. 'I knew we'd be found out.'

'Well, don't panic. Go into the kitchen, I'll deal with it.'

'Let me say it was me, they're more likely to let a woman off. And I did give them coffee the other night.'

As the doorbell rang again, Tony pushed her into the kitchen and went to answer it. The same sergeant from the episode of the fox was standing outside. He was on his own this time.

'Sorry to trouble you, Mr Chivers, but we've had a complaint.'

'Oh, yes. What sort of complaint?'

'Well, it's a bit unusual, but we have to follow these things through.'

'Of course.' He tried to sound unconcerned. 'Do you want to come in?'

'Thank you.'

'Come into my study. Bit of a mess because I've been working.'

'New book, is it?'

'Yes.'

'I've often thought you must find plenty of material around here. Some of the goings-on . . . The things we have to sort out, you wouldn't credit half of them.'

'I bet . . . Do sit down . . . This complaint . . . was it anything I could help with?' Tony sat down behind his desk and clutched his right thigh which had suddenly developed a twitch.

'Well, you might, it concerns one of your neighbours,' the sergeant said.

Tony made a show of tidying up the pile of manuscript. 'Which one?'

'The old lady four houses down, Mrs Baker.'

'Oh, that one. Yes, I've never spoken to her, but I see her out walking her dog. She usually crosses to the other side of the road when she sees me.'

'Well, she's a little odd shall we say?' The sergeant looked around and got up as Kate entered carrying a tray of coffee and some Christmas cake. 'Evening, Mrs Chivers.'

'Hello again, Sergeant. Somebody else heard the fox?'

Tony jumped in quickly. 'No, it's to do with old Mrs Baker down the road.'

'Oh, dear, thank goodness. No, I mean, goodness me, what's happened to her? Nothing awful, I hope?'

'Not really . . . Oh, thank you, you're spoiling me . . . ' The sergeant remained standing, balancing his cup and the cake. 'I was just about to tell your husband she's lodged a complaint – not the first I might add, she's a regular customer, they get queer ideas in their heads some of these old biddies . . .

last time it was one of her perennials – somebody trying to poison her dog – but the latest, and the reason I'm disturbing you, is a new one: she's convinced you've got a telescope in your attic trained on her bedroom.'

Kate's relief was so intense that she began to laugh and couldn't stop. 'A telescope in our attic?' she exclaimed.

'I agree,' the sergeant said, joining in, 'but believe me with types like her we have to follow up otherwise she's on the phone to the Chief Constable quick as a flash. I'm really embarrassed to be coming to you with this, but I promised I would make a personal search, though obviously your word will suffice.'

'Well, you can look in our attic with pleasure,' said Tony, who had become a different man. 'I'll admit I've some character faults, but peeping into Mrs Baker's bedroom with or without a telescope is not one of them. Not so far anyway. But, please, do go see, though God knows what state it's in. We haven't been up there in ages.'

'Well, perhaps I should just take a quick peep. Then I can give her a formal assurance that she's mistaken.'

'Fine. Let me show you.'

Tony winked at Kate before leading the sergeant up to the landing and pulling down the collapsible ladder. 'Careful of the cobwebs,' he said. 'There is a light, but whether the bulb still works is doubtful. The switch is just inside.'

The sergeant climbed up and poked his head through the opening. He tried the light switch and when nothing happened shone his torch in all directions.

'I tell you what you have got up here,' he said. 'A leaky expansion tank. You want to get that fixed otherwise your boiler's going to go up the spout. Same thing happened to me.'

'Thanks for telling me. Or perhaps I should thank Mrs Baker.'

The sergeant descended with cobwebs caught in his hairline. 'I appreciate your co-operation, Mr Chivers. These things are sent to try us.'

'Well, I'm sure you could have done without it too,' Tony said, sliding the ladder back out of sight. Kate was standing at the foot of the stairs as they reappeared.

'The sergeant did us a good turn, darling. He found out why the boiler's been making such strange noises. The expansion tank's sprung a leak.' In the normal course of events such a discovery would have thrown him into a black mood, but now he made it sound like a windfall.

'Once again I apologise for troubling you both. Bit premature, but a happy New Year to you.'

'The same to you and your family.'

They fell into each others' arms the moment the sergeant departed.

'For one ghastly moment,' Kate began.

'I know, don't say it.'

'You pervert. All the time I thought you were slaving over your novel, you were really taking a gander at Mrs Baker.'

'Forgive me? I'll never do it again, I've learned my lesson.'

'Shall we celebrate?'

'Let's. The thought of Mrs Baker starkers has inflamed me. Champagne?'

'In bed?'

'Where else?'

Eighteen

Twice in the space of fifteen minutes Martin drove past Patricia's house and twice his nerve failed at the critical moment. He stopped the car in a side street and once again consulted the notes he had written to himself: *Wear a suit and tie, charm the mother* (this was underlined and marked 'very important'); *don't eat before anybody else; have clean nails; polish shoes; if subject comes up try and say that the Pope is doing a great job* (careful here, in case they don't approve of present Pope); *be complimentary about everything in the house*.

He committed the various points to memory, checked his appearance for the last time in the driving mirror and moved off again, this time completing the journey. The area of Pinner where the Musgroves lived consisted of mainly mock-Georgian houses set in tree-lined roads. He noticed that quite a number of them displayed satellite dishes – the latest outward show of being with it – though, significantly,

Patricia's home did not sport one. He parked in the street, locked the car and with what he hoped was a nonchalant air, walked to the front door. There was a carved wooden nameplate fixed to the brickwork which said 'The Beeches', and under this another sign warning 'No hawkers, No circulars'. Immediately he pressed the bell a dog began to bark frenetically and a moment later hurled itself against the door. Martin took a step backwards, slipped and fell face-down into the slush that had been swept to one side of the porch. Thus, when Mrs Musgrove opened the door he was not immediately visible. She had one hand firmly holding the neck of a corgi who strained to get at Martin as he scrambled to his feet.

'There you are,' Mrs Musgrove said. 'Oh, dear, I told Kenneth to put more salt down. Don't be scared of Toffy, he's always like this with strangers, but he doesn't mean any harm.'

She dragged the dog back to allow Martin room to enter. As he wiped his feet on the mat a glob of slush came off one shoe. The entire front of his trousers was saturated and likely to give quite the wrong impression to anybody unaware of the circumstances. Mrs Musgrove averted her eyes and although she still kept tight hold of Toffy, the dog made a lunge at Martin's ankles.

'Now, stop that, Toff. Just behave. I can't scold him too much because he's such a good guard dog. Come into the lounge and meet Patricia's father.'

As he walked through a hallway decorated in a striped paper that was so bright that it strobed, he saw Patricia coming down the stairs. She pulled a face and gave the thumbs up sign before greeting him, then suddenly saw the condition of his trousers: 'Gosh! What have you done?'

'Martin had a little fall, dear, but he'll soon dry out in the warm. Unless, of course, you'd like me to lend you a pair of Kenneth's trousers?'

'No, it's nothing,' Martin said, his balls contracting from the seeping cold.

'You're very welcome, although they might be a little large for you. My husband's on the big side.'

'I'm fine, Mrs Musgrove.'

'I'll just go and infuse the tea. Pat, dear, do take him in. Is China to your liking?'

'That would be lovely.'

'Come and meet Daddy,' Patricia said. She squeezed his hand as she led him into the room. 'It's okay,' she whispered.

Mr Musgrove rose from his chair as they entered. He was a tall man, well over six feet, and wearing a formal dark suit and an MCC tie. Greeting Martin gravely, his eyes immediately went to Martin's flies, though his expression, which was not totally reassuring, did not change.

'Daddy, this is Martin.'

'Good afternoon, sir.'

'Martin had a bit of a fall if you're wondering,

Daddy.' His daughter, drawing attention to the mis-hap, produced a frown.

'Yes, I tripped just outside,' Martin explained. 'Seem to have got a bit damp.' He now could believe that his genitals had adhered to his briefs.

'No serious damage, I hope?'

'No, no.'

'Good. Come far, have you?'

'From Oxford, sir.'

'Yes, of course. Cambridge, myself, as Patricia probably told you. Do sit down.'

Martin sat on the edge of a chair while Patricia took the sofa opposite him. Whenever he caught her eye she did bright-eyed face language at him, which he found disconcerting and could not decipher. All too late he became conscious that a vital part of his strategy was missing: he knew little or nothing about her father; somehow the subject had never come up between them.

'What're you reading?'

'P.P.E., sir.'

Musgrove wrinkled his nose. 'What does that signify?'

'Politics, philosophy and economics, sir.'

'Really? Odd sort of mixture. Bit of a dead-end I would have thought. What sort of job will that lead to?'

'I haven't really decided yet, sir.'

'You said you wanted to go into public relations,' Patricia chipped in helpfully.

'Yes, that's one possibility I've considered.' He shifted carefully on his chair and crossed his legs; by now he was dying to pee.

'Public relations, eh?'

'Well, I haven't made up my mind.'

His wife came in with the tea tray. 'Pat dear, I couldn't carry it all. There are some buttered scones and a plate of lady's fingers to bring in.'

Martin had jumped to his feet, a politeness which, with Nature calling, he immediately regretted. 'Can I help, Mrs Musgrove?'

'No, thank you, Martin. Well, perhaps yes, if you could hold this while I make some room on the coffee table.'

When he had set the tray down he could delay no longer. 'D'you think I might use the cloakroom?'

'Of course, dear. The first door on the left. You'll find clean towels.'

He met Patricia in the doorway. 'Just going to use the thing,' he explained.

'Oh, right. Know where it is? That door.'

Toffy wandered into sight as he made for it, regarding him with baleful eyes. Fear released a small trickle of urine down Martin's leg. He stopped, the combination of terror and bladder control made sweat break out on his forehead.

'The dog's out here,' he called. 'Is that all right?'

Patricia came to his rescue. 'Go back in your basket,' she ordered. Cheated, the dog turned slowly, then looked back once more at Martin before retreating. Once inside the cloakroom Martin ripped his zip open, forgot to lift the seat and performed with inaccurate aim. Staring down he was dismayed to find that his crotch was an alarming shade of blue from the dye in his trousers. He snatched at the toilet roll, unravelling half of it. The holder began to play a tinny tune. He wiped the seat, then had to flush away a prodigious amount of paper. It took him three goes before the last of it disappeared and by now he had been absent a good five minutes and was of a mind never to return.

He came out to find Mr Musgrove standing in the doorway.

'Everything all right?'

'Yes. Admiring the fixtures. You've got a very lovely home.'

'Yes, we like it.'

Once they were all settled, he accepted a cup of tea and a lady's finger. 'Don't just take one, dear, they're so small. And try the ginger cake,' Mrs Musgrove said. 'Are you warm enough there? Sit closer to the fire, your hands are blue. Still, cold hands, warm heart, as they say.'

'How long before you hope to graduate?' her husband asked.

'I'm only in my second year, the same as Patricia, sir.'

'I studied for seven years before I took my articles. That's how long it took me. The things we value in life, Martin, are seldom won without effort, don't you agree?'

'Oh, absolutely, sir. These are lovely cups, Mrs Musgrove.'

'How nice of you to say so. Spode. I only use them for best. They're so expensive to replace.'

'Everything's expensive these days, isn't it?'

Musgrove said: 'And it's not going to get any better. Country's never been in a worse state.'

'Now, don't get onto politics, dear.'

'Too many civil servants telling us how to run our lives, that's the problem,' Musgrove continued, ignoring his wife. 'They've run everything else into the ground and now they're starting on the railways. My profession suffers as much as any, all the new legislation they throw at us.'

'What is it you do, sir?'

'Daddy's a solicitor,' Patricia supplied. 'I thought you knew?'

'Yes, of course I did,' he lied, 'I meant what aspect of legal work do you specialise in, sir?' The ginger cake had the consistency of plaster of Paris and clung to the roof of his mouth.

'Well, we handle a lot of litigation. Mostly domestic, I'm sorry to say. The family ethos has broken down. There's precious little respect for the sanctity of marriage any more, I find. Very depressing.'

'Yes,' Martin agreed weakly, then added: 'My parents have been married for twenty-five years.'

'How lovely,' Mrs Musgrove said. 'More tea, Martin?'

'Just a little, thank you.' He surreptitiously swilled a mouthful of tea around to try and dislodge the cake.

As she poured she gave a sly glance to her husband. 'From what Patricia's told us you and she have become great friends.'

'Yes, we have.'

'Well, that's nice. Nice for her to have a friend.'

'More than good friends, Mummy. Tell them, Martin. You've got to tell them sometime.'

Martin looked up to see if there was any comfort in Musgrove's face. There was not. His wife sat with her hands folded in her lap, with an expression that he could not fathom.

'The point is Mr Musgrove . . . Mrs Musgrove . . . as Trish . . . Patricia says . . . during the last term I . . . we found that we had a lot in common . . . and although we . . . I wouldn't . . . wouldn't . . . presume anything without your consent, the feelings we have for each other do . . . as Patricia just said . . . go somewhat beyond just friendship . . . ' He longed for either one of them to help him out or even for Toffy to reappear and attack him – anything to interrupt his stammering monologue – but nobody came to his rescue. He smiled at Patricia, hoping she might take over, but Patricia was enjoying it too much. 'That is to say,' he began again, 'or to put it another way . . . what started as a friendship has become something else . . . more . . . ' Again he gave Patricia a look, urging her to come to his assistance, but she merely nodded encouragingly, pushing him towards the abyss. Nothing he had rehearsed came back into his mind, he might have been talking in a foreign language. He saw himself tied to a post facing the firing squad with no blindfold. 'More . . . ' he repeated, then took out a handkerchief and blew his nose, 'excuse me . . . well, more than just a friendship, we find that we're in love with each other,' finally managing to get his mouth around the word. He half expected the Musgroves to be galvanised by this revelation, but nothing happened and part of his brain was signalling, *they know you've been fucking her it's written in their faces*. 'So I thought it only right that, as parents, you should know this' – the words coming faster now – 'and if you have no objection . . . I would like, we would like, we both would like, wouldn't we Pat? . . . well, to do what people do when they feel this way, and, that is . . . get married one day.'

There was a pause before Musgrove said: 'How old are you, Martin?'

'Twenty, sir.'

'And you think you could support a wife, do you?'

'I'd do my best, sir.'

Then to Martin's amazement Patricia said: 'Of course we're not in any hurry, Daddy.'

248

'No, one doesn't want to do these things in a hurry,' her mother agreed. 'But I'm sure Mr Musgrove and I appreciate your sense of responsibility, Martin. Young people these days so often just rush off without consideration for others.'

'Well . . . we are rather desperately in love, and we thought, why wait? Didn't we, Pat?'

'Yes, but what Mummy means, we have to give her time to plan everything. We certainly weren't thinking of rushing into it, were we?'

Totally baffled, Martin could only stare at her.

'Course you weren't, darling. I didn't think that for a moment. And to my way of thinking, engagements are the nicest time,' Mrs Musgrove said. She looked across to her husband. 'We were engaged for two years, weren't we, dear?'

'Had to be. Getting married is an important step, probably the most important step either of you will ever take. One has to prepare for it.'

Patricia went and threw her arms around him. 'But you're not going to object, are you, Daddy? We're quite happy to wait, aren't we, Martin?'

'Yes . . . not too long perhaps.' She's gone mad, he thought, being pregnant has softened her brain.

'These things find their own level, don't they?' Mrs Musgrove said. 'You'll find it all comes around quickly enough. Patricia would want a church wedding, of course. You might persuade the dear Bishop to officiate, Kenneth. Or at least give the blessing.' She turned to Martin. 'Kenneth is chairman of the Diocese Committee, you see, so he's very close to the Bishop. Such a fine man.' Here it comes, Martin thought, the crunch. He waited for the blow to fall. 'What church do you attend, Martin?'

'Er, Saint Saviour's,' he answered, grabbing at a name he had not used since a small boy.

'Where is that, dear?'

'Locally, where we live.'

'C of E, is it?' This said after a flick of the eyes to her husband. She did not wait for his answer, but continued, 'They seem to have got themselves in a bit of a pickle at the moment, don't they? So unlike our own church. We know exactly where we are.'

I know where I am, too, Martin thought. Deep in the *merde*.

'Would that present a problem?' Musgrove asked.

'What's that, sir?'

'Well, I have to be frank, just as you've been frank with us.'

'You see, we were expecting this, Martin dear,' his wife interrupted. 'Patricia hinted as much when she said you were coming to tea. Sorry, Kenneth, you were about to say?'

Musgrove cleared his throat. 'I was about to ask Martin if in the circumstances he'd be prepared to take instruction with a view to entering our church?'

'It would be such a comfort to us, you see?' Both Musgroves fixed laser beams on him.

'It's something you'd think about, isn't it?' Patricia said throwing him a lifebelt at long last.

'Yes, of course.'

'Father Edward is such a good man,' her mother went on. 'One might almost go so far as to call him saintly. We could arrange for you to meet him.'

Martin felt faint. This was worse than he had expected. More than their smug comments about the Bishop and Father whatsit, who he was sure would prove to be an unctuous old bore, the thing that fazed him was the change in Patricia. 'I'd look forward to that,' he managed to get out.

'First things first,' Musgrove said. 'It's always best to start with a clean sheet.'

'Oh, I'm so happy,' Patricia said. 'Shall we have a drink to celebrate?'

'It's a little early, dear.'

'And I'm driving,' Martin added quickly, wanting nothing other than to escape before he was sucked in any deeper. 'In fact, I think I must be on my way. Have to visit my grandfather in hospital.'

'Nothing serious, I hope, dear?'

'He's got mumps,' Martin said, desperately inventing a condition that sounded more serious than a sprained ankle.

Mrs Musgrove clicked her teeth. 'So painful. I hope it's not still infectious.'

251

'Oh, I'm quite safe, I've had it. But I'd better get off, the hospital's quite strict about visiting hours. Been wonderful meeting you.'

'We've enjoyed meeting you, Martin. I'm sure we shall be seeing a lot of you now. And do give our regards to your grandfather.'

He got up, his trousers, having dried, were stiff, giving him a curious posture. 'Goodbye, sir.' He shook Musgrove's hand and kissed Mrs Musgrove's proffered cheek, backing out of the room as though in the presence of religious royalty.

'Isn't it all wonderful?' Patricia said as she saw him to his car. 'Especially now.'

Something in her voice made him pause. 'Why now?'

'Because I'm not.'

'Not?' A penny began to drop in slow motion.

'What we did the other afternoon brought it on,' she said. 'I've got the curse, I'm not pregnant. So now we can have a proper wedding. I can't wait to plan it. Course, we'll have to be much more careful from now on. Don't want a scare like that again.' She kissed him and he had to exercise control not to draw back. 'They liked you. I wasn't quite sure at first, because Daddy can take against people so quickly, but you were so brilliant, I know they were impressed.'

He let her babble on, lost for any reply. A new void had opened up at his feet.

'So, we've got nothing to worry about. I bet you're relieved,' Patricia said.

'Yes. Yes, of course.'

'We had all that agony for nothing. Ring me to-night, won't you? We've got so much to talk about and plan.'

She stood on tiptoe and kissed him again.

'Say it?'

'Say what?'

'You know . . . say you love me.'

'Of course I love you.'

He got into the car, but Patricia held the door open. 'What will you tell your parents?'

'Well, you know, what's happened.'

'Drive very carefully. I know what you're like when you're excited.'

She stood on the pavement and waved until he was out of sight. Martin clutched the steering-wheel with his blue-stained hands, took the wrong turning and for a few yards drove on the right-hand side of the road until oncoming traffic hooted him and he hur-riedly corrected. In the space of an hour he had gone from being a prospective father to a Catholic convert and back again. All that bloody effort, he thought, sitting there trying to swallow that frigging cake with my balls frozen, sucking up to her mother, and now she tells me she isn't. It was too much to bear.

He pulled in alongside a public phone box and had just enough change to dial the number he wanted.

The phone rang half a dozen times before it was answered.

'Debbie?' he said.

'Yes.'

'It's Martin . . . could I come round and see you?'

As he waited for her response he saw a traffic warden arrive and start to write out a ticket.

Nineteen

Tony steered the laden trolley between the supermarket aisles thinking it was uncanny how he always managed to get one with wheels that went in opposite directions so that every few moments the thing slammed into his stomach.

'It seems only yesterday,' he observed, 'you were bemoaning the fact we still had too much food left over, so why are we buying more? Have they been giving out famine warnings on the news? Do you know something I don't know?'

'I'm just buying essentials,' Kate said, selecting a packet of a new, quilted brand of toilet-paper that had been advertised the night before. 'And some extras for Pop. I suddenly felt very guilty when we took him home. His fridge was pathetic. I think he likes these, doesn't he?' She reached into the freezer compartment and took out half-a-dozen Wonder brand steak and kidney puddings.

'Read the label first,' Tony said. 'Some of those things are packed with steroids. Before you know it he'll be growing breasts.'

'Don't be silly. They wouldn't sell them if they were dangerous.'

'That's all you know. I read an article in the *Independent* last week which said that the preservatives in TV dinners are a major contribution to violence in schools.'

'Well, he doesn't go to school, so what does that prove?'

'It proves that you have to be careful.'

'Okay, you choose then.'

'How about rabbit? I could prepare it.'

'You're not funny. I'm sick of food. Sick of buying it, cooking it, eating it. I wish they'd invent a three-course dinner in a pill. That's my idea of happiness.'

They paid and went out. 'I'm nearly out of petrol,' Tony said. 'And cigarettes.' He drove to the nearest garage. While he was filling the tank, to his horror he saw Harrison pull up to an adjacent pump in his BMW convertible. There was no avoiding him so Tony nodded and smiled. 'Have a good Christmas?'

'Splendid,' Harrison said. 'Went to the Imperial at Torquay. Do you know it?'

'Know of it, but never been.'

'You should try it one day. Beats being at home. How was your Christmas?' He seemed suspiciously chummy to Tony, since Harrison had never gone out of his way to be sociable before.

'Nothing special, just the family and a few friends.'

By now Kate was aware of the encounter. She wound down her window a fraction in order to listen in. Tony was further alarmed when Harrison didn't immediately fill his own tank but instead came over to him.

'Can you spare a minute? Have to tell you an extraordinary thing that happened while we were away.'

'Oh, what's that? You weren't burgled, were you?'

'No, thank God. But something damn peculiar. Haven't worked it out yet. Our little daughter had a pet rabbit, you've probably seen her playing with it sometimes. Thought the world of it. It was a bit of a pain actually, since I usually got landed with the job of cleaning out the hutch . . . Sure you're not in a hurry?'

'Er, no, not at all.'

'Like to get your opinion. Marjorie and I can't fathom it. You see the day we were leaving, the child went to give it a last feed and the thing was a goner, dead as a doornail. She was upset, naturally.'

Tony nodded sympathetically. 'Well, she would be. They get so attached to them, don't they? We went through it more than once when ours were young.'

'Anyway, we dried her tears, promised we'd get her another one after the hols, dug a little grave, admittedly only a shallow one because I was keen to get off and beat the traffic, but we put a cross up with Bunny's name on it, and she took it fairly well in the end. But this is the puzzling part. When we got home yesterday, first thing you know, Felicity goes to the grave to put some flowers on it, and lo and behold, grave's dug up, Bunny's gone!'

'Gone?' Tony said, somehow managing to sound genuinely shocked. 'Good God! Burke and Hare stuff. Though I've never heard of rabbit-body-snatchers.'

'Well, as you can imagine the poor child had hysterics. Course Marjorie and I told her he'd gone to the great warren in the sky, but there was no pacifying her. Cried her eyes out.'

'Understandably.'

'Took us ages to quieten her. Anyway, I trundled off to the pet shop, bought a replacement . . . but, you're not going to believe this . . . when Felicity went to prepare the hutch for new Bunny, old Bunny was back!'

'Back?' Tony said, his voice croaking. 'Back from the dead?'

'No, still as stiff as a board, but sitting up with a half-eaten carrot between its paws. Gave me quite a turn as you can imagine.'

'Well, it would anybody.'

'Marjorie and I can't fathom it. Positively ghoulish. What d'you make of it?'

'Well, as you say, baffling.'

258

'Only thing we can think of is those kids from opposite, the ones always riding their bikes on the footpath. You didn't see them hanging around our place, did you?'

'No. Mind you, we didn't venture out much because of the weather. You're probably right, though, must have been somebody's idea of a joke.'

'A joke in very poor taste if you ask me,' Harrison said. 'Sort of thing that could have scarred the child for life.'

'I hope not. They soon forget, of course, especially since you've got her another.'

'Let's hope so. Didn't want to hold you up, but I thought I'd tell you, just in case you could throw any light on it.'

'Sadly, no. But I do sympathise. What a start to the New Year.'

'Yes, last thing one needed. Well, nice to see you. We must get together one of these days. I've been thinking of starting a neighbourhood watch.'

'Good idea,' Tony said. 'There are some odd characters around.'

Harrison finally went back to his car. Tony hurriedly paid and drove off. 'Did you hear all that?' he said as soon as they were out of the forecourt.

'Did I ever!' They both started to scream with laughter. 'I didn't dare look at you,' Kate said, eyes streaming. 'How did you manage to keep a straight face? I bet you're relieved.'

'And how. God, when I think of the lengths I went to, making old Bunny lifelike. He was a work of art by the time I'd finished, even though you thought I was insane.'

'You were insane.'

'First time Harrison's ever seemed vaguely human.'

'Well,' Kate said, still laughing, 'it takes a tragedy like that to bring people together. Didn't you love that bit about the great warren in the sky?'

'Classic. You can start being nicer to Emily now. She was falsely accused.'

Twenty

Mysteriously, most of the snow had disappeared overnight; only a few sculpted blocks of grey ice remained on the lawn, reminding Tony of the sort of creations that usually won the Turner Prize. There was a soggy bounce under his feet as he ventured out for a morning constitutional before commencing work. The English climate held a perverse fascination for him; he had a love-hate relationship with it; hating the way in which it could give one a glimpse of perfection and then, arbitrarily, snatch it away – blasting the magnolia blossoms with a sudden frost, producing freak hailstorms on the best of the summer days so that the roses were flattened, or else organising a drought during the spring so that, bewildered, everything germinated a month too late. On the other hand he loved the surprise element, the fact that everyone was so grateful for any prolonged period of good weather, giving rise to smiling exchanges between complete strangers who would otherwise pass by with heads averted as though fearful of being mugged by a greeting.

The garden was his domain. Kate liked to look at it, but bemoaned the money he spent on it every year to stop it reverting to a weed-ridden bomb site within the space of days. Over the years they had suffered at the hands of half a dozen jobbing gardeners, who all began well, but inevitably became more trouble than their hourly rate justified. Kate put it down to the fact that neither she nor Tony knew how to handle staff; they hadn't been born to it and, overwhelmed with gratitude when they actually succeeded in finding a treasure, went too far in the opposite direction, so that, within a very short space of time, their staff's inadequacies were readily accepted, the employer/employee roles reversed: the gardener's lumbago preventing him from doing any heavy digging, or the cleaning lady's sciatica precluding her carrying the vacuum upstairs. Terrified that any criticism would mean a total withdrawal of labour, Kate would do the heavy tasks herself and settle for some desultory dusting, while Tony would excuse the fact that the greenhouse contained nothing but a petrified forest of unripened tomatoes if the lawn got mowed. He had often remarked that the only thing every one of these bogus Fred Streeters could cultivate were gigantic marrows – possibly the most dreary vegetable known to man – and dahlias, a flower that Kate refused to have in the house. It was a costly battle that was never won, and in addition to the casualties wreaked by human hands, there were other battalions lying in wait, for the animal world had also singled them out as easy prey. Despite Emily's effort to reduce their numbers, tribes of grey squirrels stripped the bark from the trees, passing the time in mindless acts of destruction, until the exact moment when the apples ripened, when they pillaged those; squadrons of wasps holed every single plum and something chillingly named 'black spot' attacked the roses, while Nature, anxious not to appear prejudiced, sent a mist of white flies to ravage anything under glass. Every known species of bird, gifted like those manic escapees who once inhabited Colditz, penetrated his fortress soft-fruit cage to feast on the raspberries, leaving only the gooseberries which, in any event, were of a variety that yearly proved too sour to eat. He could remember only one triumph when, purely by chance, he had succeeded in growing three melons, the size of tennis balls, from seeds bought in France.

'Why do you bother year after year?' Kate would ask. 'Settle for a few window boxes and pots near the house, and let the rest go wild.'

Although, in his heart, Tony agreed, he could not surrender. Born and bred in a town, he had a misguided faith in his ability to beat the rap, seeing himself as a latter-day Thoreau creating his own

Walden, battling on even when reason told him the cause was lost. He had also never fathomed why, during those rare years when certain things came good, he managed to produce a surfeit of vegetables at the very moment they were giving them away in the shops. If the truth were known he had been conned, together with the rest of his fellow countrymen bent on the same hopeless horticultural pursuits, into believing they were destined to till the land, that an Englishman and his garden were, like Siamese twins, joined at the hip, never to be parted.

Part of his angst stemmed from the fact that Harrison, who had some poncey job in the City, could afford to spend a fortune on a high-powered firm of landscape gardeners who arrived like paramedics, resuscitating the near-dead and bringing the neighbouring plot to nauseating perfection – Harrison's manicured grass greener, his flower beds a riot of colour, his trees exquisitely shaped, Beauty alongside the Beast. Once a year Harrison threw his garden open to the public in a blatant display of one-upmanship; hordes of middle-aged ladies, clucking like hens, perambulated around Harrison's Eden, averting their eyes from Tony's desert beyond the fence.

Now as he plodded across his own mossy lawn to search for any sign of the three hundred early crocuses he had planted, Tony was ready to admit defeat. Perhaps Kate had the right idea: let the whole thing revert to the jungle, give the weeds *carte blanche*. Nothing in two decades had killed them, even though he had used enough pesticides to put the entire Green Party into intensive care. Once he had resorted to a flame-thrower, a piece of machinery he had never fully mastered, which seared the paths, but seemed to revitalise the weeds after a week.

He stopped and listened as the wail of an air-raid warning being tested cut through the distant noise of motorway traffic. Why the hell did they still religiously do that after nearly fifty years? Were there still people wearing steel helmets painted white who had never been told about VE Day, but were still holding out like those Japanese the Yanks found on a remote atoll long after everybody else had committed hara-kiri? Even though he had never experienced the Blitz, the sound had a chilling effect, first the fluctuating warning note then the continuous All Clear. Perhaps it has something to do with preserving the memory of our finest hour, he thought. The British liked nothing better than an orgy of nostalgia, anything that perpetuated the myth of the sceptred isle standing alone. For some obscure reason a bawdy version of a childhood poem came into his mind, a parody considered unbelievably daring during his last term at school. *They're changing guard at Buckingham Palace, Christopher Robin's gone down on Alice.*

He stood looking at the still frozen pond, smiling to himself at the memory, then picked up a stone and fractured the ice to give those goldfish spared by the heron a chance to survive for its next visit. Shivered by a sudden gust of wind, he returned to the house, his optimism dented but not extinguished. There was always another year, things might improve.

'I'm back,' he shouted from habit, rather as though he had returned from a long absence instead of a walk through the Paradise garden. The house now had a peculiar silence to it, the only sound the click of the dishwasher as it moved to the drying cycle. 'I'm back,' he repeated, then saw the note Kate had left clipped to a milk carton, placed where even he could not miss it. She had gone to the hairdresser's and would be back in an hour.

He felt a sudden rush of loss, Kate's temporary absence disorientating him; he had intended to tell her something important and now it would go from him. A withered sprig of mistletoe had fallen to the floor outside his study. He picked it up and carried it to his desk. The beginning of a new year was stripped of any immediate expectations, he thought, the tangled sacred and profane rites of the holly and the ivy and the virgin birth were over, one just had to stumble through January as best one could. Only the very rich can order the seasons like a succession of wonderful meals. 'We who are left have no choices,' he said aloud.

He enjoyed the freedom to chain-smoke while Kate was out, re-reading for the umpteenth time the slew of manuscript pages, delaying the moment when he must start work on it again. He welcomed the arrival of the post, any excuse to delay switching on the computer. His mail that morning included an invitation to find his perfect partner, two handsomely produced brochures urging him to take out insurance for his old age, a calendar from a builder whom he hadn't employed for a decade, two charity appeals, a once-in-a-lifetime offer for an authentic reproduction of El Cid's Toledo sword, a reminder from the dentist that he was overdue for a visit, two bills stamped 'Please Pay', a wrongly addressed Christmas card, and finally a letter from his brother. Roger had always had the habit of running his written thoughts together, his cramped handwriting sloping from north to south-east across the pages.

'Dear Tony,

   Sorry I gave you such a hard time over Christmas, at the start I sensed a strong odour of disapproval, understandable in many ways. Maybe our long-overdue talk cleared the air. I hope so. I'm trying to reconcile my emotional balance sheet, a step not without pitfalls as you can imagine, and where this will eventually take me is anybody's guess at the moment, but I thought you should know that Vanessa and I have pulled back from divorce and are having a trial separation, what the Brazilians term a desquite.' (Roger had once

267

spent a week in Rio, visiting a client putting some distance between himself and the Inland Revenue, and ever since he was apt to use isolated Brazilian words.) *'I believe our paths may converge again, especially if she finds it possible to embrace my new faith. Thank Kate for her hospitality and the sweater. Roger.'*

'Poor old sod,' Tony said. He put the rest of the mail to one side and sat at his computer to resume work on his unfinished novel. Eventually, after two or three false starts, he wrote a few sentences that pleased him and as the morning wore on he slowly roused his reluctant imagination, plotting the fates of his characters with more ease than he could organise his own life.

That same morning Martin awoke in an unfamiliar bed. Coming out of a dream he sat upright and bumped his head on a low ceiling. For an appreciable moment afterwards he had no idea where he was; nothing that came into his blurred field of vision was recognisable. Normally, the first thing he saw every morning was a stained patch of flowered wallpaper. It was only when he attempted to get out of bed that he became dimly aware that he was not in his college digs and that he appeared to have grown a spare limb during the night. His right leg was entangled with a third, a warm, slightly clammy entanglement that finally nudged him from the last remnants of sleep. Gingerly reaching beneath the bedclothes, he traced a path along a leg that was not his own until he arrived at a furry junction. Only then did he turn to look. Deborah was asleep beside him.

Dim recollections began to take shape in his mind. Of course: he had come to her flat to pour out his heart after the Musgroves' Mad Hatter's tea party, and what with one thing and another, mostly another, helped along by the remains of Deborah's lethal punch, it had developed into something that in his wildest dreams he had never thought possible but which now, as the memory returned, was probably not only predestined but, in the execution, had been extremely rewarding.

Deborah stirred as he sought to free his cramped leg from hers. She turned towards him, one of her hands flopping to rest on a sensitive spot where other angels had often feared to wander. Gently disengaging her hand he rolled off the bed, stooping so as not to bash his head on the ceiling a second time. Descending the ladder, he stepped over their strewn clothes and went into the tiny bathroom. After relieving himself, he sluiced his face in cold water and used Deborah's toothbrush – not something mother would approve of, he thought, but then she wouldn't approve of the rest either. He examined a purple love-bite just beneath his shoulder blade and found scratch marks on one of his forearms. He was branded. Who would have thought it? That surprising Deborah had burned brightly in the forests of the night. He relived their frantic coupling, a feeling of unalloyed satisfaction creeping up on him. You've got some thinking to do, he mouthed to himself in the mirror. *Quo vadis?* Fresh emotions diminished the guilt he felt towards Patricia, though the speed with which his feelings had changed towards her was still slightly shocking. He started to make himself believe she had led him up the proverbial garden path; maybe the entire episode had been a trap to ensnare him? It was not unknown, was it? Girls could be as predatory as men in getting their own way, everybody knew that.

He wandered the few steps into the kitchen and opened the fridge. Deborah's revealed an interesting collage of her personality: a packet of frozen Mars bars, several cans of diet Coke, a half-empty bottle of white wine, a jar of instant coffee, a slice of curling melon, two pieces of fried chicken wrapped in cellophane, an unopened pizza and, thankfully, a loaf of bread. He put the bread in the toaster and boiled a kettle for the coffee, and was still standing there, happily bemused by events, when he heard Deborah thump down the ladder. As naked as himself, she presented a rosy, Renoiresque vision that immediately steered his thoughts away from breakfast. Love in the morning seemed the icing on the cake.

'I'm making toast and coffee,' he said, his eyes fixed on her breasts.

'So I see. I like the new look for fast-order chefs.'

'D'you think it'll catch on?'

'I could live with it.'

She yawned, then put pliant arms around him and offered her lips.

'Well, what about us?' she said, as the long kiss finished.

'What about us? You sorry?'

'No . . . except for Pat.'

'Oh, so am I,' Martin said quickly. 'But, I mean, neither of us planned it, did we? It just happened.'

'I guess I won't be her best friend for much longer.'

'I certainly won't. But we don't have to tell her all right away, we could let it come out gradually.'

They were still standing close to each other and he again thought how deceptive girls' clothes were. Last night, seeing her body revealed for the first time, had been exciting enough, but now it made him ache to possess her again, an idea which occurred to her in the same instance.

'Hang on a sec,' she said. 'Must go to the bathroom.'

He climbed the ladder again, breakfast forgotten, and lay waiting for her. He heard her shower, the delay intensifying his anticipation. She came back into view still wet, like a naiad rising from the sea, to sit astride him, holding herself a few teasing inches away until the game proved too unbearable for both of them. Her expression changed, her eyes closing as she lowered herself onto him. Martin's hands fluttered on her damp, arched back as he pulled her closer, wanting the soft contact of her breasts on his chest as her hair, red like the colour behind his eyes, fell across his face.

Twenty-One

'Nobody rang while I was out?' Kate asked as she plonked a cup of coffee on Tony's desk.

'What? Oh, thanks. No, nobody.'

'I thought one of them might have rung. How's it going?'

'So-so. I haven't worked myself back into it yet. Always the same when I don't go at it every day.'

'Read it to me, that often helps you.'

'I will later. Have you done something different to your hair?'

'Yes, I suddenly felt the urge to have a few inches chopped off. D'you like it?'

He swivelled round and studied her. 'Yes. Nice. I thought you'd been out a long time.'

'But do you really like it?'

'Yes.'

'You don't sound too sure.'

'Yes, it's . . . makes you look . . . I always prefer

you with long hair as you know, but it looks good.'

'I knew you wouldn't like it. I said to Michael you wouldn't.'

'No, I do, I do, I just wasn't expecting it, that's all.'

'Well, it'll soon grow again. Did you make yourself a sandwich?'

'Not yet. I haven't stopped.'

'I'll get you one.' She looked at herself in the mirror, thinking, to hell with it, I'm not mad about it either, but I'm not going to say so. 'Funny Jenny hasn't phoned to tell us if they're coming home this weekend,' she said as she was leaving the room. 'Hope there hasn't been any change.' She went out and immediately returned. 'You know it's Twelfth Night, don't you? We must get the tree down today otherwise it's bad luck. Will you help me later, I can't do it on my own?'

'Sure. Just say when. I wouldn't mind a break.' The phone rang at that very moment and he waited to see if Kate picked up before printing his morning's work and switching off the computer.

'I give up on that son of ours,' Kate said as he joined her in the kitchen.

'Why, what's happened now?'

'I thought he was ringing to tell us how he got on with Patricia.'

'And was he?'

'No. Not in the way we expected. She's not having a baby and she's history. That was how he put it:

"she's history." '

'Why?'

'Don't ask me. To think what he made us go through, ruining Christmas, all that agonising for nothing. He's the bloody end. I put the phone down on him.'

'Well, let's be relieved he's not going to make us grandparents just yet. At least that's a plus.'

'Oh, shoot! Now look what I've done,' Kate said. 'I've put marmalade on your cheese sandwich instead of mustard.'

It has to be the saddest sound in the whole world, Jenny thought, as the young bugler played the Last Post. The thin notes seemed to hang in the dank Belfast air for ever. She held herself stiffly, trying not to cry as she saw Andy come to attention and hold a salute. Instead of returning home straight away, he had insisted on staying to attend the funeral. Three of the dead members of his platoon had been transported home to England to be buried, but the fourth had been a local boy, scarcely twenty. She stood alongside his grieving family, the mother supported by two of his brothers, one of them holding an umbrella over her with his free hand. As the final bugle notes sounded, a detachment of the dead soldier's company, lined up on both sides of the open grave, were given a barked command by a senior NCO and brought their automatic rifles up to the firing position. A further command and then six staccato shots rang out. The echoes bounced off the cemetery walls, and a flock of crows, disturbed by the reports, flew cawing into the leaden skies. When the firing party had been marched away, the family and mourners shuffled forward to sprinkle earth on the coffin. Jenny remained where she was, thinking that could have been me, seeing herself held by her mother and father and the long emptiness that would have remained.

The formalities over, Andy rejoined her.

'Are you okay?' she said. He nodded in reply, still conscious that he was on view. She wanted to take his arm, but wondered if that was allowed while he was in uniform. Instead they walked side by side to where Andy's driver waited by his car. They spoke very little on the journey to the barracks. There, Andy changed into mufti and this time, for security reasons, they were driven in an unmarked car to the airport to catch the London plane. Andy had already told her they had been booked under false names, a further reminder of the life he had lived and which, for the past week, she had briefly shared.

It wasn't until the plane had gained cruising height and set course for England that she was finally able to relax and think about the secret she was carrying home.

Denuded of everything except the angel, the tree had a forlorn look.

'I hate this job,' Kate said. 'It always depresses me.'
She wrapped each glass ornament in tissue paper and put them away carefully in boxes. The tree lights had been wound around the cardboard tube of a spent toilet-roll. 'You have to do it that way,' she told Tony, 'otherwise they won't work next year.'

'They didn't work this year,' he said.

He started to vacuum the carpet of fallen needles, but she stopped him. 'Don't do that yet. Waste of time until you take the tree out, but get my angel down before you do it.'

He climbed the step-ladder and untwisted the picture-wire that had held it in place.

'Are you really going to preserve this thing for another year?' he said.

'Of course. Don't be horrid about it. You won't throw away your decomposing teddy-bear.'

'He's an heirloom. Bears like that go for a fortune at Sotheby's.'

'Then sell him, we could do with the money.'

Tony loosened the retaining screws on the contraption that had held the tree secure and hoisted it free. He took it through the french windows. Outside, he lopped off the branches and then hacked the trunk in half. Like turkeys, Christmas trees got a raw deal, he thought.

Going back inside the house he couldn't find Kate at first, finally tracing her to the bedroom. She was sitting on the bed, crying, the angel in her lap.

'Now what?' he said.

'It's all right, don't worry, I'm not crying. We've just had some good news, that's all.'

Tony sat beside her. 'You gave me a shock. What good news? Tell me.'

'Jenny,' she said, 'they're both home safely, thank goodness, and guess what, she's pregnant.'

Later that night, alone in his study, work abandoned, Tony sat thumbing through the book Evelyn had given him for Christmas. One sentence in particular caught his eye, 'The dread of loneliness is greater than the fear of bondage,' Connolly had written, 'so we get married.' Gifted, cynical Connolly – had he written that warning, like any of us who live by the pen, to leave a footprint on the printed page to show that we have passed this way, Tony wondered, or merely for effect?

It isn't true of me, is it? he thought, putting the book to one side as the silence of the night was broken by a vixen's scream coming twice, far away. But this time he felt no panic, instead, a curious, comforting affinity. He guessed she was searching like everybody else for some way to survive, just a small gift in a world that portioned them out sparingly.

He poured himself a whisky and switched on the computer. His words appeared out of a blue void, as did glad tidings and bad news, the only difference being there was no 'Delete' key in life. Nothing was

278